A SONG TO REMEMBER

KAY CORRELL

ROSE QUARTZ PRESS

Published by Rose Quartz Press

022619

This book is dedicated to all the people who understand the magic of music. The way a song can transport you back in time, bring back a memory, make you stop and just...
listen to the melody.
And to all my choir nerd friends in high school... you helped bring the magic of music to life.

KAY'S BOOKS

Find more information on all my books at
kaycorrell.com

COMFORT CROSSING ~ THE SERIES

The Shop on Main - Book One

The Memory Box - Book Two

The Christmas Cottage - A Holiday Novella
(Book 2.5)

The Letter - Book Three

The Christmas Scarf - A Holiday Novella
(Book 3.5)

The Magnolia Cafe - Book Four

The Unexpected Wedding - Book Five

The Wedding in the Grove - (a crossover short

story between series - with Josephine and Paul from The Letter.)

LIGHTHOUSE POINT ~ THE SERIES
Wish Upon a Shell - Book One
Wedding on the Beach - Book Two
Love at the Lighthouse - Book Three
Cottage near the Point - Book Four
Return to the Island - Book Five
Bungalow by the Bay - Book Six

SWEET RIVER ~ THE SERIES
A Dream to Believe in - Book One
A Memory to Cherish - Book Two
A Song to Remember - Book Three

INDIGO BAY ~ A multi-author sweet romance series
Sweet Sunrise - Book Three
Sweet Holiday Memories - A short holiday story
Sweet Starlight - Book Nine

Sign up for my newsletter at my website *kaycorrell.com* to make sure you don't miss any new releases or sales.

CHAPTER 1

Sophie Brooks was in trouble. Big trouble. She'd promised more than she could deliver, and failure didn't sit well with her.

She dropped a handful of paperwork on her desk in the back room of Brooks Gallery. Right now she had an art show coming up and only one artist displaying his work when the event had been billed as a multi-artist show. Her art show was part of the Autumn Arts Weekend in Sweet River Falls. She'd promised she'd hold a multi-artist showing at her gallery with the artists present for the opening.

That wasn't going to happen.

It had been bad enough when Lance Jones had pulled out. His wood carvings always drew a crowd as well as his personal appearances. He was charming, funny, and told wonderful stories about the pieces he carved. But she understood. His mother was ill, and he had to go to California to take care of her. He'd left her a few pieces of his work for the show, but it wasn't the same as having him here in person.

Then Belinda Morgan had pulled out because she said it wasn't worth her time if Sophie couldn't deliver some other big-name artists.

Not that Belinda was much of a big name herself...

Lovely. Just lovely. And she had just two weeks to solve her problem. If there was even a solution. How could she find any artists to come here and display their work on such short notice? Shows were booked months in advance, if not more, not at the last minute. It made her look like she didn't know what she was doing.

And maybe she didn't.

If her mother were still here, she'd know what to do. Her mother had been able to charm everyone. No one would ever have dared pull out of one of her mother's art shows.

But she wasn't her mother, as clearly seen by this failure she had on her hands now.

She rubbed the back of her neck and cocked her head from side to side. She needed a solution, and she needed it fast.

She stared at the wall across from her desk as if it would give her an answer. The wall replied with stony silence.

"I DON'T NEED A VACATION." Chase Green practically spat the words into his phone. "I'm fine."

"You're not fine. You're snapping at everyone. You're going to lose your favorite backup guitar player, not to mention the fiddler. You hate changes to the lineup of musicians who accompany you."

"I do," Chase admitted. He raked his hand through his hair. He needed a haircut, but he *didn't* need a vacation.

Sam, his manager-slash-agent-slash-friend, continued, "You need to go away for a bit. We don't have anything scheduled for the next few weeks."

And that was a problem, too. *And* it was more than just a few weeks. He didn't have another gig for eight weeks.

Eight weeks.

Not even a smaller one in some lousy venue.

He just needed…

He sighed. Maybe Sam was right. Maybe he should take a break. He couldn't remember the last time he'd taken any time off. Even if he wasn't on the road, he was busy recording or writing music or promoting.

"All right, fine. I'll take a short trip. But make sure I don't lose those musicians."

"Great. I'll see you back here in, let's say, three weeks." Sam sounded relieved.

"Two. Maybe sooner." Chase clicked off his phone and shoved it into his pocket. He looked around at the walls of his apartment that he'd just recently moved into.

He scowled.

Well, it had actually been about a year ago when he'd moved. He didn't have a darn thing up on the walls. A single table with two chairs sat by the window. His bedroom had a bed, an old wooden crate for a night table, and a lamp with a crinkled lampshade.

He was hardly ever here. It wasn't like he needed the place to be all jazzed up. Maybe he should just stay here this week and fix it up. Try to live like a regular human being.

No, sitting around in this lousy apartment was no way to spend a couple of weeks.

A man his age should live in a nicer place than this. Own some nice furnishings. Things certainly hadn't turned out like he'd planned. He glanced at the gold-plated record in a frame, resting against the wall. It seemed like an eternity since he'd gotten that. Though, to be honest, he felt like he only deserved half of it. Or maybe even less than that.

He crossed into his bedroom and pulled out a battered suitcase. Now, where the heck was he going to disappear to for a couple weeks? Or maybe just *one* week...

BETH CASSIDY HURRIED through the Brooks Gallery to the back room where she knew she'd find her best friend, Sophie. She felt kind of guilty that she and Sophie hadn't been spending as much time together since she and Mac had become... well, boyfriend and girlfriend. Though boyfriend and girlfriend seemed like silly terms for people their age.

Sophie had invited her over for a quick drink tonight. Beth had missed their happy hours spent sipping a glass of wine in Sophie's loft above the gallery. She only had about forty-five minutes until she was meeting her mother and the boys for dinner, but she'd been determined to at least stop by for a quick visit.

"Soph?" Beth poked her head into the office.

"Hey." Sophie turned and gave her a warm smile.

It didn't fool Beth. She could immediately tell something was wrong by the stressed look in Sophie's eyes. "Hey, yourself. And what's wrong?"

"Nothing's wrong."

"Nice try." Beth walked over and hugged Sophie. "Spill it."

"Well, I've promised a multi-artist show for the Autumn Art Weekend."

"I saw the flyer. The town has a lot going on that weekend. Always nice to try to pull in more tourists in the offseason. Hope it doesn't snow…"

"My artists have cancelled. Well, two of them."

"Bet one was that snobby Belinda."

Sophie tossed her a wry look. "Yes. She pulled out after Lance had to cancel. Though, his mother is ill and he's leaving to go be with her. I don't fault him for that."

"Well, we'll just have to find you some other artists."

"It's just two weeks away…"

Beth frowned. "That's not much time, but I bet we can figure something out. You're showing your work, aren't you?"

"My jewelry isn't really art."

"Of course it is. And you heard Mac when he saw it. He thinks you're very talented, so it isn't just your best friend telling you that you are." Beth grinned, then snapped her fingers. "Hey, what about that photographer? The one Mac said he loved his work so much? Hunt, somebody."

"Hunt Robichaux? I do have some of his work still for sale here. I wonder if he would be willing to come here for the show. Maybe bring some more photographs." Sophie's brow creased. "That might work… if he's available. His photos of the mountains and the river are amazing. He has a great eye and a remarkable talent for capturing unique angles and lighting."

"There, that's one. It's going to work out, trust me."

Sophie gave her a grateful smile. "When have I ever not trusted you?"

"Smart woman." Beth laughed as she and Sophie headed upstairs to the loft for their quick happy half-hour.

They settled into two comfortable chairs by the window overlooking Sweet River. Sophie kicked off her shoes. "So, how goes the mayor race?"

Beth's relaxed attitude fled out the window. "It's… going. Sometimes I wonder…"

"If you're crazy for running for mayor?" Her friend grinned at her.

"Well, I'm pretty sure I am crazy for running, but it's something I need to do. We need to get someone in there who isn't just one of Old Man Dobbs' buddies, doing his bidding."

"I hear you on that, but your life is already crazy busy with your teaching job, the boys, and now dating Mac. No one would blame you if you pulled out of the running."

"Not happening. I can figure out a way to make it all work. I have to. Besides, Mom is great with helping me with the boys. Mac is super supportive of… well, of everything."

"He's a great guy. I'm glad you two worked things out."

"I'm sorry I've been so busy that I haven't had much time to drop by. I miss our happy hours." Beth looked down on the river walk behind Sophie's loft. A couple walked by, hand in hand in the low lights from the streetlights that were just beginning to illuminate the walkway. How many times had they sat in this very spot, talking or just sitting quietly?

"I know you've been busy. We just have to do what we have to do, right?"

Beth frowned. "I guess. But sometimes it would be nice to have more time to do what we want to do, instead of getting bogged down in what we *need* to do, wouldn't it?"

"We've got responsibilities. Nothing we can do to change that."

"Yeah. When did we become adults, anyway?" Beth laughed. In her mind she still pictured Sophie and herself as young, carefree high schoolers.

"I'm not sure how it happened." Sophie nodded agreeably. "Kind of just crept up on us, I guess. We're not those same two carefree kids running around in high school, or convinced that studying for exams in college was the most excruciating, overwhelming responsibility we'd ever have."

Beth raised her glass and clinked with Sophie's. "To adulting. May we both survive it."

CHAPTER 2

Chase wasn't sure what made him remember a vacation from his childhood, but memories had suddenly flooded his mind in broken detail. One of the last fun family times he could remember. He, his parents, and his brother, Garret, had gone to a small town in Colorado and stayed at some lodge there.

The memories had convinced him. He'd thrown his hastily packed suitcase and guitar in his car and headed out from Nashville to Sweet River Falls. He'd stopped somewhere in Kansas to spend the night to break up the eighteen-hour drive. By the end of the second day, he wondered why he'd picked a place so far away from home. If he could even call Nashville home. He was used to road trips. He'd made enough trips on the bus with the band, but then he wasn't the one driving.

He finally pulled onto Main Street in Sweet River Falls and parked his car. He couldn't quite remember how the town looked all those years ago, but it was charming now. Like the kind of small town you'd see on a postcard. The town bustled with people walking along the sidewalks. A sign on a nearby storefront proclaimed the best coffee in Sweet River Falls.

He stretched as he climbed out of the car and turned his face to the afternoon sun. That's what he needed. Coffee. He entered Bookish Cafe. A lady with a friendly smile greeted him. "Welcome."

"Ma'am." He nodded at the woman.

She set down a stack of books she was carrying. "Can I help you find something?"

He looked around at the display of books but nodded toward the counter across the room. "I'm looking for some of that best coffee in Sweet River Falls."

She grinned at him. "You've come to the right place." She held out her hand. "I'm Annie."

"Nice to meet you."

"Lindsey over there will get you some coffee." She nodded toward the counter.

"I was wondering…"

"Yes?" Annie looked at him.

"Well, when I was a young boy, I came here with my family. To town, I mean. We stayed at a lodge. It was on a lake and if I remember correctly, it was also right by a river. They had a bunch of cabins and a big dining room to eat at. I don't suppose you'd know the name of it?"

"You're in luck." The woman's eyes twinkled. "That's Sweet River Lodge. My best friend still runs it. Nora Cassidy."

"I thought I might try and get a cabin there for a few days."

"Go grab yourself a coffee, and I'll call Nora and see what they have available."

He walked over and got a tall black coffee. Their sign in the window wasn't far from the truth. It *was* an excellent cup of coffee. He took a few sips and waited for Annie to finish her call. She came over to where he was browsing through a book on hiking trails in the area.

"Got you all set. Here are directions." She handed him a piece of paper. "Cell service is kind of spotty around here, so even if you put the lodge in on the map on your phone, there's no guarantee you'll get service well enough to follow along on your app."

"Thank you, I appreciate this."

"No problem. I'm not surprised you remember the lodge. It's kind of a magical place. Nora has a lot of repeat customers who come back year after year."

He didn't know if he remembered it as magical, but it had been one of the last places his family had enjoyed a normal life. Before everything had exploded and their world had been turned upside down.

A strong yearning to return to that simpler time pulled at him. Maybe he'd find the peace he was looking for at the lodge.

Or not.

He finished his coffee, said goodbye to Annie, and hurried back outside, eager to see the lodge again.

CHASE PULLED up to Sweet River Lodge as the late afternoon sun sprinkled golden rays across the lake. The place looked different than he remembered. More cabins. A bit more updated in a rustic kind of way, not that he was one hundred percent sure of his memories of the place. He climbed out of the car into the chilly Colorado air. A tangy scent of pine trees and fresh earth drifted on the breeze. He followed the signs to the office and went inside to register.

"May I help you?" Another friendly face.

"Annie from Bookish Cafe called?"

"She did. I have a cabin all ready for you. I'm Nora, by the way."

"Chase. Chase Green."

The woman didn't react to his name, which wasn't that surprising. He'd been half of The Second River Bridge band, but Kimberly Day was the name that most people remembered. She'd been the memorable one with her long blonde hair, charismatic voice, and effervescent personality.

He filled out the registration information, gave her his credit card, and took the offered key. "It's cabin fifteen, Rustic Haven. We just finished remodeling it. It has a nice view of the lake."

"Sounds perfect."

"How did you hear about us?"

"I actually came here with my family when I was a boy."

Nora smiled at that. "Love to hear that. Something about this lodge calls people back." She handed him a simple map of the property and showed him where his cabin was.

"Thank you."

"Have a good stay. The dining room is open if you're looking for a good meal. Miss Judy, our cook, is fabulous."

"Might just take you up on that." He nodded and headed back out to his car.

He parked in front of cabin fifteen, then went inside with his guitar and suitcase. The small cabin had a kitchen that opened to a family room. One small bedroom and a bathroom were off to one side. The cabin had pine-planked ceilings and freshly painted warm white walls. It even had a few pictures and decorations, unlike his own apartment back in Nashville. A huge picture window framed a beautiful view of the lake, just in time for sunset.

It took him all of five minutes to unpack, then he looked around the cabin.

Now what was he supposed to do?

The clock on the wall ticked through the silence.

SOPHIE STOOD on Nora's front porch. Beth's mom had invited her to dinner, and she never could refuse Nora's home cooking.

"Come on, Miss Sophie. Won't you sing for us?" Trevor pleaded with his bright blue eyes shining at her. How could she refuse her best friend's son?

Sophie smiled and ruffled his blonde hair. "You bet, Trevor. Just a few songs until it's time for dinner. Go get your mom's old guitar from the closet."

Sophie had tried numerous times to teach Beth how to play the guitar over the years, but Beth had finally given up, announcing it wasn't one of her stronger talents.

No kidding. Beth had been all thumbs. But she'd kept her guitar stashed at her mother's cabin, and Sophie often used it to sing for the boys. Lullabies when they'd been little, nursery rhyme songs as they'd gotten a bit older, then expanded into many other types of music as they grew up. They were always an appreciative audience.

Beth came out of Nora's cabin and sank onto the porch swing. "Mom says dinner will be ready in about fifteen minutes. I'm not allowed to help her with anything, but she did seem to approve of you keeping the boys occupied while she finishes up."

Trevor came back out with the guitar with his brother, Connor, close behind. "Here you go."

The boys settled onto the porch swing, one on each side of their mother. Sophie pulled the guitar from the case and strummed the strings. She adjusted a couple of them until they were back in tune.

"Okay, what do you want me to sing?"

"That song about living down that old dirt road."

"Chalk Road?"

"That one." Trevor nodded vigorously.

She'd written that song years ago after visiting Annie's father at his house on Chalk Road. That was back when he'd been alive and living in the house. She could only imagine growing up in a home like that, and her thoughts had taken wings like they often did when she started to write a song, and the words had poured from her as she'd jotted them down on an old scrap of paper. Years later, it was still one of her favorite songs she'd written.

"Good choice." Beth nodded and slowly pushed the swing with one foot.

Sophie strummed the guitar and launched into the haunting melody of Living Down Chalk Road.

CHAPTER 3

C hase should have grabbed the map of the property when he'd left the cabin. He thought the dining room was this way, but now he wasn't sure...

He stopped dead in the middle of the pathway. The unmistakable strumming of a guitar mixed with the silvery voice of a woman singing threaded its way through the trees. Her voice flowed like a river around him, pulling him in its current. He turned and headed in the direction of the song as if it were sweeping him along with it and he had no choice.

He stopped by a clump of trees and spied a woman sitting on the porch of a cabin at the far end of the property. Another woman and two boys sat listening to her. He edged closer. Her words held them all spellbound, him included.

He stood behind the trees as she finished her song, unable to walk away, unable to interrupt the intimate group.

"Hey, look. Hi, mister." One of the boys jumped up and waved to him.

Feeling unbelievably guilty at being caught spying on them, he stepped closer into the warm porch light spilling out onto the ground in front of the cabin. "I'm sorry. I didn't mean to interrupt. I was headed over to the dining hall and I heard the music."

"I hope I didn't disturb you." The singer stood, one hand holding the neck of the guitar.

"Not at all. It was quite good."

"Thank you."

Chase could swear he could see her blush in the muted glow of the porch light.

"Do you want to join us? Sophie's going to play some more, aren't you?" The other woman gestured to him.

"I don't want to bother you."

"Not at all. Everyone loves to hear Sophie sing."

The Sophie woman tossed a what-are-you-doing frown toward the other woman.

He usually wasn't so uncertain. Should he join them? Would it bother Sophie if he did? Was that what her frown was about? In a split instant decision, in spite of his doubts, he crossed the distance, climbed the stairs to the porch, and leaned against the railing. He wanted nothing more than to hear this woman sing again.

"I'm Beth, this fabulous singer is Sophie, and these rascals are Trevor and Connor, my sons."

"Nice to meet you. I'm Chase."

"Go ahead, Miss Sophie, sing us another one." The younger boy piped up.

Sophie settled back on her chair and picked up the guitar. A self-conscious look swept over her face. "I... uh... what should I play?"

"Play the one about the two little girls." The older boy—whichever name was his had been lost on Chase—urged Sophie.

She sent Chase a quick look, then bent her head over her guitar. After a few opening chords, she started into a delightful, upbeat song about two best friends. Little girls who became lifelong friends. Once again her voice swept around him, enchanting him. The quality of her voice and the clever words held him in her spell. Rarely did music move him like this anymore.

But this woman, this Sophie, her voice... he could listen to her sing all night long.

As the song ended, the younger boy jumped up and clapped. "That's about you and Momma, right?"

"It is, Trevor." Sophie nodded.

Ah, the younger boy was Trevor, so the older boy must be Connor.

"That was really great." Chase turned to Sophie. "*Really* great. So you wrote that song?"

"I did." She blushed again. This time it was quite evident, even in the low light.

"Do you sing professionally?"

"Oh, no. Just here and there."

"She's wonderful, isn't she?" Beth bragged on her friend.

"She really is." He couldn't argue with that.

A woman opened the door and peeked out. Nora. The woman who owned the lodge. That's who she was.

Nora looked at him and smiled. "Oh, Mr. Green. Nice to see you. I guess our Sophie's voice caught your attention."

SOPHIE LOOKED up and scanned the man's face in the warm porch light. Chase. Mr. Green.

Her mouth dropped open. Chase Green.

That Chase Green?

He'd been listening to *her* sing.

The heat of a full-on blush flushed through her.

Chase pushed off the railing. "Yes, I admit. I heard her singing and had to come over. I was looking for the path to the dining room but must have gotten lost. Glad I did. Sophie has a wonderful voice."

"That she does." Nora agreed. "Would you like to join us for dinner? I have plenty."

"Oh… I don't know." He looked tentative.

"Say yes." Beth got up from the swing. "Mom always makes enough to feed half the county. We'd love for you to join us."

"If you're sure."

"We're sure." Beth smiled at Chase.

Sophie sat like some kind of idiot, frozen in place, unable to move. *Chase Green.*

"Come on in, then." Nora beckoned to all of them. "Dinner's ready."

The boys rushed inside, and Chase followed after them.

Beth got up, walked over, and shot her a quizzical look. "You okay, Soph?"

"Do you know who he is?" She whispered the words.

"Mr. Green?"

"Chase Green." She said the words slowly and watched for a spark of recognition to enter Beth's eyes.

Beth frowned. "Chase Green. Should I know him?"

"He was part of Second River Bridge."

"Huh?" Beth looked truly confused.

"The group. That country duo. Chase Green and Kimberly Day."

"*That* Chase Green?" Beth's eyes widened.

"That's what *I* said." Sophie got up and grasped the guitar in a tight grip. She'd been singing for Chase Green.

CHAPTER 4

B eth and Sophie entered Nora's cabin, and Sophie placed the guitar in the corner. They crossed to the dining table, and Chase flashed her a smile. The smile he was known for. That and his deep, throaty voice. She should have recognized his voice when he first spoke. Distinctive, rich, mesmerizing, with just a hint of southern drawl.

She could still feel the heat on her cheeks and knew she had her telltale blush plastered across her face. Chase was used to listening to professional singers. Accomplished singers. Not just some woman who occasionally sang a song or two to entertain friends or maybe at a local event.

"Hey, everyone. Are we late?" Beth's

brother, Jason, came into the room. Mac McKenna trailed behind him.

Sophie watched as Beth's face lit up when Mac entered. He crossed over and placed a quick kiss on Beth's cheek.

"Hey, Mac. You made it." Trevor pulled out a chair next to him. "Come sit by me."

She glanced over at Chase, who looked a bit stunned by the sudden swarm of people around the large dining table. She recognized the deer-in-the-headlights expression. She didn't blame him. It sometimes overwhelmed *her* to come take a place at Nora's table, and she was invited often.

"Chase, take that seat. Sophie, why don't you sit next to him?" Nora pointed to two chairs. "Come on, everyone. Sit down. Don't want the food to get cold."

Chase held out a chair for her, and she gave him a tentative smile. Chase Green. Holding a chair for her. She slipped into the chair and grabbed her napkin. The napkin that she promptly dropped on the floor.

She reached for it, and she and Chase bumped heads.

"Oops, sorry." His voice, that deep voice. He

handed her the napkin, looking directly at her with his warm brown eyes.

She dropped it once more like a toddler playing will-you-pick-it-up-again. This time she reached down swiftly and grabbed it herself and carefully, ever so carefully, placed it in her lap.

Chase sat down beside her, and the noisy chaos that was dinner at Nora's began.

CHASE TOOK another helping of the delicious beef stew as well as another thick slice of homemade bread. He hadn't had a home-cooked meal in… well, he couldn't remember the last time. His cooking skills were nonexistent, and he usually just grabbed something to eat on his way home from work, which was often very late at night.

The constant laughter and good-natured teasing at the table was like sitting in a foreign country to him. A big family meal. It was all just so unfamiliar to him but tickled at some long-forgotten memories.

But he enjoyed it.

Probably.

But it sure might take some getting used to.

But it didn't really matter because it was a one-time invitation. He'd happened to stumble upon this family and their friends, and they'd done the neighborly thing by inviting him to their meal.

Sophie intrigued him, though. Not only her voice but the easy way she talked to Beth's kids and the way she tossed back teasing remarks to Beth's brother. Everyone at the table seemed so at ease.

Beth smiled at him from across the table. "It's a bit of a free-for-all when we get together, isn't it?"

"A bit overwhelming, yes."

"Mom loves to have a big family dinner with friends, too. Hope we're not too much for you."

"Not at all." Which was a bit of a fib...

The man sitting next to Beth—Mac, wasn't it—leaned over and said something to Beth. She smiled back at Mac, and he reached over and squeezed her hand. Chase had been watching them during the meal. They were obviously in love and not afraid to show it.

Sophie caught him watching Beth and Mac and leaned close to him. "Don't mind them. Young love." She grinned.

"So I see." He couldn't take his gaze away

from Sophie's blue eyes. They held him captive almost as tightly as her voice had when she'd been singing.

"I've got cake and pie for dessert." Nora stood up and began to clear away the plates. Sophie jumped up to help, unfortunately taking her eyes with her.

"I'll help." He stood.

"Nonsense. You're company. Sit," Nora commanded.

He did as he was told, but a momentary pang of loneliness filtered through him. Company. He wondered what it would feel like to actually belong to this group.

After a flurry of activity with clearing the table, dessert was served. Soon he was eating the most delicious slice of apple pie he'd ever had. Or maybe it was the company. Did most families get together like this? Was this a normal thing for most people? He thought meals like this were just on those sentimental holiday movies his mother used to love to watch. The ones that always had a happy ending and ended with a kiss. He quickly dismissed the memory.

"Did you get enough to eat?" Sophie looked at him with those sparkling eyes of hers again.

"More than enough. It was wonderful." He pushed back slightly from the table.

"No one goes away hungry from one of Nora's meals."

Beth stood. "Mom, let me help with the dishes, then I better be getting the boys home. School night."

"I've got dish duty tonight, sis. You go ahead and wrangle these monsters home." Jason stood and gathered a handful of plates.

"Hey, I'm not a monster," Trevor insisted.

"It's just an expression." Connor rolled his eyes with exaggerated older brother impatience.

Chase stood, unsure whether he should offer to help again or get out of the way and let the family get back to their lives.

"I should go, too." Sophie got up and grabbed her plate and coffee cup.

Taking a clue, Chase did the same with his. He followed her into the kitchen, placed his dishes on the counter, and turned to Nora. "Thanks so much for having me."

"My pleasure."

Beth poked her head in the kitchen. "We're out of here. Thanks, Mom."

"I best be heading out, too." He turned to leave.

"Sophie, why don't you show Chase out?" Nora gave Sophie a quick hug. "Come back soon. We always love to have you."

Sophie hugged her back. "Thanks for the invite." She turned to him. "You ready?"

Sophie grabbed her coat from the hook by the door and was surprised to feel Chase holding it for her as she slipped into it. "Thanks."

He opened the door for her, and they slid out into the chilly night air. They walked off the porch, and he looked up at the sky.

"A million stars out here, aren't there?" She watched as he stared at the dark night surrounding them, broken only by splinters of starlight.

"I sure don't see skies like this in the city."

"Where do you live?" Though she was pretty sure he was going to say Nashville. Didn't all country singers live there?

"Nashville."

Of course. "Are you just taking a vacation?"

Chase laughed. "You could call it that. It was highly suggested to me to get away for a bit.

My manager, Sam—he's also my friend—thought I was getting a bit… testy."

"Everyone needs a break every now and then." Though she couldn't remember the last time she'd taken any time off or gone on vacation. Not in years. The gallery kept her too busy.

"I guess." He didn't sound like he was convinced.

She still couldn't believe she was standing here, *right here*, with Chase Green and having a normal conversation. Though it didn't *feel* normal.

"Well, I guess I should call it a night." His deep voice washed over her. She could listen to him talk all night. But of course, that wasn't going to happen.

"Yes, me, too." But she just stood there next to him.

He looked up at the stars again, then back at her. "Do you think you'd like to maybe go walk by the lake before you leave? Do you have time?"

"I've got time." Her heart fluttered. She was going to take a walk with Chase Green. The night was unraveling like some kind of romance novel, not that she was complaining.

They wandered down the path from Nora's cabin to the lake and settled onto a bench beside the water. The moonlight danced across the ripples in the lake.

"This is a mighty fine view." His deep voice wrapped around her.

"It is." She looked up at the stars twinkling in the heavens and for the umpteenth time in her life thanked those lucky stars for allowing her to live in such a beautiful place. Though, at times, she wondered what it would be like to travel around. See other towns, other cities. Under these very same stars, but from a different perspective. But Sweet River Falls was where the gallery was, and it was her responsibility to run it.

They sat in silence for a while. A comfortable silence, which surprised her. She should be nervous sitting beside someone so well known, but he had a way about him. A comfortable presence like a favorite quilt.

Sophie turned and studied his profile lit only by the moonlight. He sat relaxed, staring out at the lake, lost in thought. Feeling a bit like a groupie for staring at him for so long, she finally broke the silence. "So, are you planning on staying here at the lodge for long? Or are you just passing through?"

"I'm not sure. I haven't made definite plans. Going to stay here at least for a few days, though. Do some poking around."

She almost offered to show him around town but couldn't quite make herself actually say the words. She admitted she was a bit star-struck with just sitting here with him. And he'd listened to her sing. The telltale heat of a blush crossed her cheeks yet again. He must just have been being nice to say she had a wonderful voice. At one point in time, she thought music would be her life. She'd even taught music at the high school. But that was before... It seemed like a long, long time ago. It had only been five years, but it seemed like forever. Life had a way of throwing curves at you. She stared at a leaf floating across the water, propelled helplessly by the gentle breeze, unable to change its course. She could so relate to the one lone leaf.

"Well, I should probably let you go." Chase stood, pulling her from her thoughts.

She stood also and took one more look at the lake. "I should be going. I've got a long day tomorrow."

"I had a nice evening. Your friends were

very nice to invite me for the home-cooked meal."

"Nora loves to feed people."

"I'm glad I was here to be fed." He grinned at her.

"I… I better go."

"Let me walk you to your car."

"I. Uh. Okay." She sounded like an idiot. She turned and led them down the path to where she'd left her car near Nora's cabin. She opened the car door and stood there. "Well, thanks."

"Night, Sophie."

"Good night, Chase." She slipped into her car and drove away. Away from a night she'd play over and over again in her mind. She knew she would. The night she'd sat by Lone Elk Lake with Chase Green.

As she drove down the lane, she regretted not offering to show him the town. She might never see him again.

CHASE WATCHED as Sophie drove away and the red taillights disappeared around a curve in the road. He turned and headed back down the path to his cabin. It had been an interesting evening, to say the least. He'd had a great time, even if he'd felt a bit out of place at Nora's dinner table. Not that they were anything less than welcoming.

And then there was Sophie.

Sophie of the sparkling eyes and enchanting voice.

And he hadn't even caught her last name.

CHAPTER 5

Sophie struggled to shrug out of her jacket and dropped her keys on the counter as she dug in her purse to grab her cell phone.

"Hello?" She contorted around to allow the jacket to slip to the ground.

"I talked to Jason and he said he saw you and Chase down by the lake when he was walking back to his cabin tonight." Beth's voice came across the airways.

"He did?"

"Yes, spill it."

"There's not really anything to tell."

"Right. You both just happened to wander down to the lake at the same time?"

"No, he asked me to go for a walk." She bent down and picked up the jacket.

"And?"

"And we sat by the lake and talked for a bit. He seems... nice."

"Nice? That's all I'm getting? What did you talk about?"

"The view, the stars."

"Did you tell him you knew who he was?"

Sophie walked over to the coat closet and hung up her jacket. "No, I didn't really know how to bring it up. What was I supposed to say? Hey, I know that you're *that* Chase Green?"

"That would have been a start. You going to see him again?"

"I don't know. I mean, I could run into him again, I guess."

"Really, Sophie, haven't I taught you better than this? You could have asked him to stop by the gallery. Or asked him for coffee. Or—"

"Why would he want to have coffee with me?" Sophie grabbed her keys and hung them on a hook by the door. A small attempt to keep order in her life.

"Because you're funny and good company and he loved your singing. Hold on just a sec..."

Sophie heard Beth's voice from a distance. "Connor, I told you. Time for bed. I mean it."

"Sorry, I'm back. The boys are a bit wound up tonight," Beth continued.

"I couldn't just ask him to come by the gallery."

"Sure you could."

"Maybe I could have Mom mention to him that you own the gallery and tell him where it is. I bet he'd stop in…" Beth's voice held a conspiring tone.

"Beth, stop it. It was just a chance meeting. A one-time thing."

"If you say so. Just a sec again—"

Sophie smiled as she heard Beth's voice in the background, chasing the boys to bed.

"Soph, I better go. I'm going to read to the boys and hopefully, they'll settle down. I have some schoolwork to grade, then I'm headed to bed."

"Okay, good night. And thanks for inviting me over to Nora's."

"You're always welcome. Anytime, you know that. And I still think you should have asked Chase to stop by."

"Good night, Beth." She rolled her eyes, set her phone on the counter, and walked over to the window. She flipped off the lights in the apartment and stood in the darkness, watching the river bubble over the rocks in patches of light from the street lamps along the river walk.

Maybe Beth was right. Maybe she should have asked Chase to stop in and see the gallery. That would have been a natural thing to ask. Just being friendly and neighborly to someone new to town.

No, who was she kidding? A famous person from Nashville wasn't going to be interested in her and her predictable, same-same life. A woman who didn't even seem to be able to make good on her promise of a special in-person art show for the Autumn Arts Weekend. She'd left multiple messages for Hunt Robichaux, but he hadn't returned her calls.

No, it was best that she just had this one memory of a night with Chase Green. A memory she'd keep for years to come.

BETH FINALLY GOT the boys into their pajamas and tucked into bed. "Okay, what should we read tonight?"

"The book about the boys camping in the

mountains. You know, by themselves. Without their Mom and Dad." Trevor jumped out of bed and ran to the bookcase. He grabbed the book and climbed back into bed.

"Okay, but you know that you guys can't ever go camping without me, right?" She wasn't sure this *do an adventure without your parents* was a good idea to plant in their minds.

"We know, Mom." Connor's voice held exaggerated patience like he was talking to a two-year-old.

"But I think it would be fun. I'm sure Connor and me could camp alone."

"Connor and I."

"No, Connor and me… no parents."

"She was correcting your grammar, stupid."

"Don't call your brother names." Beth sighed and leaned back against the headboard on Trevor's bed. "Okay, a couple of chapters, then it's lights out."

"Thanks for reading to us tonight." Trevor cuddled close to her. "You don't do that much anymore. You're too busy."

Beth leaned down and kissed the top of Trevor's head. He was right. She needed to make more time for simple moments like this.

"I'll try to make more time, Trev. I will." She didn't know how she was going to keep that promise, but she'd find a way. There was nothing more important to her than her boys.

CHAPTER 6

Keely Robichaux looked up from clearing a table at the end of the early breakfast rush at Magnolia Cafe. The sunshine poured through the open door as her husband, Hunt, entered the cafe.

His eyes lit up when he saw her, and her heart swelled at the sight of him. He'd been out of town on an assignment, photographing a hot air balloon lighting for a regional magazine. She hadn't been able to go with him like she usually did because her sister, Katherine, had been sick and unable to look after the cafe they jointly ran.

He crossed over and swept her into a big hug. "I missed you, Mrs. Robichaux."

She leaned her face up to be kissed. "I

missed you, too." She still wasn't used to being called by her married name.

"Kat, feeling better?"

"I am." Kat rolled up behind them in her wheelchair. "So, are you glad to be back in Comfort Crossing? Going to stay for a bit?"

"Well, if you're feeling well enough to run the cafe, I thought I'd ask my beautiful bride if she wanted to take a little trip."

"Where?" She perked up at the prospect of a trip.

"I finally got around to checking my messages after I got back into a good cell phone reception area. I got asked to do a show in Sweet River Falls, Colorado. Remember that gallery that has a few of my photos? The owner asked if I'd like to bring more work and do a personal appearance. I thought maybe you'd like to go? She apologized for it being so last minute, but it sounds like she's in quite a bind. I wouldn't mind a trip to Colorado. How about it?"

Keely turned to her sister. "You okay if I leave again? I feel like I've been taking so many trips with Hunt and leaving you here to deal with everything."

"I thought that was our deal? You travel as

much as you want. I run the cafe. You know I enjoy it." Kat's eyes were warm with encouragement.

"I thought you might want to do an article on the town while we're there. They're having an Autumn Arts Weekend." Hunt smiled at her. "I can photograph the town and the festival, you can write up an article.'

She reached out and touched his face. "I'm in."

"How about we make it a road trip? That way I can bring some framed prints with me. You up for that?"

"That's a marvelous idea. You know I love a good long road trip." Especially with Hunt. He always made their trips fun and exciting. She loved her new found freedom to travel now that Kat had taken over so many responsibilities at the cafe.

"Then it's a go. I tentatively told the owner, Sophie Brooks, that I'd come. But said I had to check things out to be sure. I'll call her now and tell her it's a go."

"Why don't you and Hunt go home now? I've got the cafe. I'm sure you two want some time alone after him being gone so long."

Hunts eyes twinkled, and he winked at Kat.

"Thanks, Kat. You're the best sister-in-law ever."

A warmth spread through Keely and she smiled. At her sister, at her husband, and at the life she now had. She had to be the luckiest woman in the world. "Kat, you really are the best."

"And don't you forget it." Kat waved them away. "Go. Enjoy yourselves."

Keely took her husband's hand in hers, and they walked out into the warm Comfort Crossing, Mississippi sunshine.

CHASE DROVE into town the next morning to take a look around. Besides, that best cup of coffee in Sweet River Falls was calling his name. He parked on Main. The street was already bustling with activity. First, he was going to get that coffee, then he was going to hit the outfitter shop and buy some hiking boots. He might as well get out into the mountains while he was here.

He walked into Bookish Cafe and Annie greeted him. "Welcome back."

"Your coffee was calling my name."

"We have some nice pastries, too, if you'd like one to go with your coffee."

"That sounds great." He ordered his coffee and a hearty looking cinnamon roll covered with pecans and took them to a table. The local newspaper was on the table, so he glanced through it while he ate. There was a big article about the upcoming Autumn Arts Weekend. Looked like a fairly big deal for the town. Exhibits, art showings, an arts and craft fair, and a big concert.

He read through the names of the performers at the concert. He'd heard of a few of them. A couple rising country singers. He always tried to keep up with the new competition. Their headliner was Jackson Dillion. He had a few records out and was starting to get more well-known. A young kid, a pretty fair performer, and Chase thought Jackson was probably going to make it in the biz.

Maybe if he were still here that weekend, he'd go and hear the concert.

Nah, he couldn't imagine he'd still be around in two weeks. He folded the paper carefully and got up from the table. He browsed around the bookstore, looking for a guide to hiking trails in the area. He found one that had them listed by difficulty and rated the views along the trail. Perfect.

He went to the counter to check out.

"Oh, that's a great little book," Annie said as she reached for it to ring him out.

"I thought I might do some hiking while I'm here."

"If you're looking for an easy hike to help you get used to the altitude, you could try the trail to Lost Lake. The view is beautiful as you climb over the pass then dip down to where the lake is nestled between Skyview Mountain and Grace's Peak."

"Thanks for the recommendation."

"You'll need something better than those cowboy boots to hike in."

"I'm headed over to the outfitter's shop right now."

"Good plan. There's a dusting of snow up there, I hear." She handed him the book. "Come back again."

"I'm sure I will." He left the shop and hurried down the street to Alpine Outfitters. He soon left the shop with hiking boots, warm socks, a warm down jacket, and a backpack. He should be all set. He was beginning to feel like a real mountain man. Maybe he could fit in here after all.

He juggled his packages as he headed back to his car. As he walked down the street, a black and white photograph caught his attention in the window of a gallery. The lighting through the trees and the sparkle of the sun's rays on the water were expertly captured in the photo. He recognized the view. It was Lone Elk Lake. This time bathed in sunlight instead of moonlight. A sign next to the print said the photographer, Hunt Robichaux, was coming for a full showing and appearance at the Autumn Art Weekend. He was tempted to go to the showing, not that he had a single photo or painting on his walls. He wouldn't mind having *this* photo on his wall. It reminded him of the time he spent with Sophie. Her face kept popping up in his thoughts...

But, once again, he reminded himself that he probably wouldn't be here by the time the Art Weekend rolled around anyway.

CHAPTER 7

Sophie looked out the window and saw Chase standing and staring at Hunt's photograph. She could almost feel Beth shoving her out the door, even though her friend was safely ensconced at the school at her teaching job right now. She took a deep breath and hurried over to the door. One more deep breath and she was outside.

"Morning."

Chase looked at her and smiled. "Well, good morning."

"I see you're admiring Hunt's work."

"I am. He's done a great job with the lighting on this one."

"Did you see that he's coming for a personal appearance at the Arts Weekend?"

"I saw that."

"You should come." Now, what made her blurt that out?

"Oh, I don't know if I'll still be around then."

A momentary pang of disappointment tweaked at her, which was silly. She'd just met him. Sat by the lake with him for a few moments. Why would she feel disappointed if he didn't come to the showing?

"Do you work here?" Chase juggled his packages.

"It's my parents'. I mean, mine. I... well, I took over for them." She never quite felt like it was actually *hers*. She still thought of it as her parents' gallery. "Would you like to come in?"

"I was just going to drop these packages at my car."

"The outfitter's, huh? Did Chuck try to sell you the store?"

"Pretty much." Chase grinned. "Tell you what. I'll go dump these in my car and come back and see the gallery."

"Sounds good." Sounded really good. Though, really, she shouldn't be this pleased about him coming to see the gallery, should she?

"I'll be back in a few minutes."

Sophie watched him walk away, then turned to hurry back into the shop, rubbing her arms to warm up from the chilly air.

She looked around the gallery, moved a few things, and basically waited in anticipation of Chase's return.

Which was silly.

He returned in a few minutes, and her heart raced as he walked in the door.

Which was *also* silly.

He walked up to her. "So, do I get the personal tour?"

The words hung in her throat. "Ah…" She cleared her throat. "Sure."

"Do you have more of Hunt's work?"

"That's the last one, but he's bringing more. He's actually coming to town in a few days. He said he was bringing his wife, and they're going to combine a short vacation with his appearance at the show." She was so relieved that Hunt had said yes to a personal appearance. She would still like to find someone else, but at least the show wouldn't be a complete bust. And Hunt's work was excellent. He'd be sure to draw a good crowd.

"I saw a flyer about the weekend. Looks like

your town has a little bit of everything planned."

"I admit, Sweet River Falls does love its festivals and shows. Seems like we have at least one a month. More in the summer when we're packed with tourists. I seriously keep a calendar in my office to keep track of all of them."

She led him over to a glass display case.

"That's a nice-looking necklace and bracelet." Chase pointed to the pieces displayed in the cabinet.

A blush heated her cheeks. "I... uh... I made those."

He turned to look at her, his eyes wide with surprise. "You did? Those are great. You're very talented. Singing and an artist. Wow."

"Oh, I wouldn't really call myself an artist."

"Well, I would." Chase nodded emphatically.

Sophie intrigued him.

It had been his good luck that he'd run into her as he wandered down the streets of Sweet River Falls. He'd been ruing the fact he hadn't asked her out or made some kind of plans to meet up with her again.

He wasn't going to make the same mistake twice. "So, I was wondering… would you like to go out while I'm in town?"

She turned her head away from him for the briefest moment. Ah, here it was coming. She was seeing someone, or getting over a bad relationship and had sworn off of men, or maybe she just wasn't interested in him.

Though, he'd thought they'd made some kind of connection while they sat by the lake last night, but what did he know about women? He'd sworn off of them himself.

She turned to look at him and gave him a tentative smile. "I'd like that."

"Really?" He couldn't keep the surprise out of his voice. He'd already decided she was going to turn him down. He wasn't very good at this dating thing.

"Yes, really."

"Great. Dinner tonight?"

"Dinner sounds nice."

"So, how about you recommend the place since you're the expert on Sweet River Falls."

"There's Antonio's Cantina. Mexican food

and really great margaritas. It's just down the street."

"Antonio's it is. What time should I pick you up?"

"Seven works for me."

He turned to leave. "Oh, wait. Where do you live?"

She pointed one finger up to the ceiling. Up above the shop."

"That's convenient."

"It is."

"Okay, I'll see you at seven."

Chase went out into the bright sunshine and whistled as he headed back to his car. She'd said yes, and he was ridiculously happy about that.

SOPHIE KEPT LOOKING at her watch, waiting for school to be over so she could call Beth. A group of customers came in mid-afternoon and kept her busy. She thought they were just window-shoppers, but they ended up buying two paintings and one of her silver jewelry pieces.

She glanced at her watch as they left. Beth should be finished teaching now. The door opened to the shop again and she sighed. First, she'd wait on the new customer. She turned around and grinned. "Beth."

"Hey, you. Thought I'd stop by for a few minutes."

"I was just getting ready to call you."

"But my intuition told me to come by instead." Beth walked over and gave her a quick hug.

"Guess where I'm going tonight?"

"No clue."

"I'm going out with Chase Green."

"You asked Chase out?" Beth's eyes widened.

"No, he asked *me* out." Sophie shook her head. "We're going to Antonio's."

"It would probably be obvious if I went and got a table in the corner and spied on you guys." The corner of Beth's mouth raised in a teasing smile.

"Probably." Sophie rolled her eyes.

"So much for that plan."

"It was all kind of a coincidence. I saw him out the shop window. He was looking at Hunt's photograph so I went out to talk to him. Oh, and guess what else? I heard back from Hunt. He's coming to town for the Art Weekend."

"Well, you've had a pretty fabulous day, haven't you?"

"So far," Sophie agreed. She'd had a great day. A date with Chase and she'd gotten an artist for the show.

"You have to call me tonight when you get home and tell me all the details."

"I'm getting kind of nervous about it."

"Why?"

"Well, he's a famous country singer and I'm just... me."

"You're just talented and fabulous and pretty and he's lucky to go out with you." Beth's voice had a fierce protective edge to it. She paused and looked critically at Sophie. "Now, what are you going to wear?"

Sophie looked down at her practical skirt and blue blouse. "I hadn't gotten that far." What did a person wear on a date with a country singer?

"How about that new teal sweater you bought when you went into Denver last month? It looks great with your eyes. And your skinny black jeans. Oh, and your cowboy boots with the teal stars on them."

"Well, just like that, my wardrobe is planned." Even if it didn't stop the butterflies in her stomach and the ridiculous giddiness that flowed through her just thinking about this evening. Which was silly. Really silly. And yet… it was there.

"I'm a full-service best friend, just sayin'."

Sophie gave her a hug. "You're the best friend ever."

"I've got to run, but seriously, call me when you get home tonight. No matter what time. I want to hear every little detail." Beth turned and started out of the gallery. She paused when she got to the door. "And, Sophie, relax and have fun."

Sophie waved. She fully intended to have a great time. If she could just get over feeling so nervous.

She looked at her watch again. Melissa was coming in soon to work and she'd be closing the gallery tonight, so Sophie should have time to get ready before Chase came to pick her up.

Chase Green.

Chase Green was coming to pick her up for a date…

CHAPTER 8

C hase couldn't remember the last time he'd had a date. Oh, he'd gone to some events with women. Places he was supposed to be seen. Parties he needed to attend. Sam was always urging him to network. But he hadn't gone out on a date-date... just him and a woman, just the two of them, in forever.

That must be why he was so nervous.

So *very* nervous.

More nervous than when he first stepped out on stage. Well, the kind of nervous he *used* to feel when he stepped out on stage. The *last* time he'd stepped out on stage... well, that had been a nightmare.

One he wasn't going to think about now.

He'd stopped by a florist in town and picked

up a bouquet to give to Sophie. Now he was wondering if that had been the right decision. He was so rusty with his dating skills. But all women liked flowers, right? He hoped so. He'd gotten a bouquet of yellow roses with some kind of lacy looking white flowers in with them.

He entered the shop, not knowing how to get upstairs to Sophie's apartment. A woman finished talking to some customers and came over to him. "You must be Chase. Sophie said to send you on up. The stairs are in back." She pointed to a door in the rear of the gallery.

He crossed the expanse of the gallery past cleverly arranged displays and opened the door at the back. He entered a small alcove with another door to the outside. The stairs rose off to the left. He took a deep breath, ignoring his racing pulse, and climbed the flight. With each step, he told himself not to be so nervous.

It appeared he wasn't listening to himself.

When he got to the upstairs landing, he knocked on the door. The knock echoed through the nook at the top of the landing.

Within moments, the door opened and Sophie stood in the light spilling from inside. He swallowed. She wore a teal sweater that positively lit up her eyes. Black jeans hugged her long legs. Two silver bangles caught the light on her left wrist. He wondered if she'd made them.

"Hi." She smiled at him.

"Hi." He stood there like a fool. He glanced down at the flowers. "Oh, here. These are for you." He awkwardly thrust them toward her. Very gallant. Not. He tried to hide his nervousness behind a smile.

"Thank you. Come in and I'll put them in water."

He followed her inside and looked around the apartment. The loft was open from the kitchen to a great room to a couple of comfortable chairs in front of a huge picture window on the back wall. A cozy afghan draped over a couch, and a rocking chair that practically begged a person to sit on it was placed near a reading lamp. She had artwork on her wall, of course. A varied mixture that somehow all tied together in perfect harmony.

Her loft was warm, inviting, and such a contrast to his sparse apartment. He made up his mind right then to fix up his apartment when he made it back to Nashville. There was no reason he lived like some penniless college student.

He followed her to the kitchen area and

stood by the counter. She pulled out a white glass vase from a cabinet and arranged the flowers. "The vase was my mother's. She collected milk glass everything. Vases, plates, bowls. I kept most of her pieces."

He wasn't sure what milk glass was exactly, but he could see a variety of white vases and bowls in the open cabinet.

"Thank you so much for the flowers. They're lovely." She placed them on a small cafe table in the corner. The table had two chairs with bright, comfortable-looking cushions. He could see her touch in everything. The furniture, the decorations, even the subtle warm color of the walls.

"Your apartment is nice. It all looks so... comfortable." Was that an okay compliment to make? Was comfortable a compliment? Should he have said pretty? Or well put together? *Could he get any more awkward?*

And now he was talking to himself.

In his mind.

This was crazy.

"THANKS." Sophie looked at the flowers on the

table, then moved the vase an inch to the right. Much better.

Chase still stood in the same spot in the kitchen. Should she ask if he wanted a drink? No. Maybe if they left and went to Antonio's, the noise and friendliness of the restaurant would make her feel less skittish?

"You ready?" His rumbly voice rolled through her loft. She was pretty sure she could sit and listen to his voice talk about anything he wanted to talk about.

"I'm ready. We can just walk. It's not far."

"Fine by me."

She grabbed her jacket and Chase helped her slip it on. She flipped out the lights, and they headed down the stairs and out the back door. "We can walk down the river walk, then cut across Main when we get to the courtyard area."

She headed down the pathway beside the river with Chase at her side. The rumble of the river as it poured over the smooth rocks did little to soothe her jangled nerves. She should say something, anything, but her mind went blank. They walked on in silence until they reached the courtyard.

"We cross here, then Antonio's is right down that side street."

He took her elbow as they stepped off the curb at the corner, but quickly let it go as they crossed the street. Even though she ignored it, she could imagine she still felt the heat on her elbow from his momentary touch.

They continued to Antonio's, and Chase opened the door for her. She slipped inside, still searching for words.

"Sophie. So good to see you." Antonio walked over and kissed her cheek. "And who is this?"

"Antonio, this is Chase."

Antonio reached out his hand. "Nice to meet you, Chase. You two follow me." He led them to a booth in the corner.

Sophie slipped into the booth, and Chase sat across from her. She took the menu Antonio handed her even though she didn't need it. She knew everything on the menu.

"Margaritas to start?" Antonio looked at them.

"Yes, for me." Sophie nodded.

"Sounds good to me, too." Chase looked up from his menu.

They ordered their meals and sipped on

their drinks. She didn't know why she was having such a hard time talking to him.

Sure she did. He was a famous singer, and she was just... Sophie Brooks. No claim to fame.

She noticed a few people in the restaurant glancing over at them. They recognized Chase, that much was obvious. She couldn't help but wonder if they were speculating on why he was here with *her*.

As if to prove her point, Gloria Edmunds walked up to the table. "Hello, Sophie."

"Hi, Gloria." Gloria was about the last person she wanted to see.

"Aren't you going to introduce me to your friend?"

"Chase, this is Gloria. Gloria, Chase Green." Why had she added his last name? Maybe Gloria hadn't recognized him?

"Mr. Green. It is *so* nice to meet you. What brings you to Sweet River Falls?" The look on Gloria's face plainly showed that she didn't think that Sophie was the reason Chase was here.

"Just taking a little break."

"Here in Sweet River Falls? I would think you'd be vacationing somewhere more exciting."

Way to support the town, Gloria.

"I'm actually enjoying the slower pace. I'm staying at the lodge on Lone Elk Lake. It's very nice."

"Nora's place?" Gloria's face held a mask of barely disguised disapproval. "Oh, well. If you decide it's too *rustic* there, a new really nice hotel went in just outside of town. The Bellingham. It's very elegant and chic."

Gloria said the word rustic like it was the most contemptible term ever.

"I think the lodge is lovely. The perfect place to stay." Sophie defended the lodge. Gloria had always had some kind of grudge against Nora, but Sophie wasn't having any of it.

"I guess. If you like plain and… simple. Not many luxuries like I'd think Mr. Green would be used to."

"I'm actually enjoying my stay there. It's peaceful and the view is great."

"I guess." Gloria didn't look convinced.

"Well, enjoy your dinner, Gloria." Sophie hoped Gloria would take the hint.

"Oh, I just came in for a margarita."

"Okay, then enjoy your drink." Sophie gritted her teeth.

"Mr. Green, if you'd like me to show you

around town, I'd be happy to." Gloria dropped a business card on the table.

"Uh, thanks for the offer." He shot Sophie a quick look.

"There's not a lot to see, but there's a really nice restaurant near the event center. The chef there is excellent. I could get a reservation if you're interested. I'm sure you'd enjoy the food there much more than Antonio's."

"Sophie says the food here is great."

Gloria laughed. "Well, it's okay."

Sophie began to worry that Gloria would never leave.

"Well, it was nice meeting you." Chase smiled at Gloria.

Gloria tapped her business card laying on the table. "Call me." She turned and walked away without saying another word to Sophie.

"Well, she was... interesting." Chase's face held a quizzical expression.

"Gloria is something. She has this rivalry or something going on with Nora. Not sure what started it. But she thinks she's better than Sweet River Falls. She moved to Denver for a while but moved back. I'm not sure why, since she obviously thinks so little of the town." Sophie stared at the business card on the table, wanting to take it and crumple it in a wad of paper.

An awkward silence drifted over the table while Sophie sat and ranted about Gloria in her mind.

"So, the Autumn Art Weekend. Do you have it every year?" Chase set his drink on the table.

Finally, a topic she could launch into. "We do. I think it's been about twelve years now." Her mother was involved in planning the first one. It had grown over the years. Sophie tried to do right by her mother's vision for it and threw herself into the festivities every year. "It draws a lot of people to town. All the shops participate in some way. We have food trucks with all kinds of fabulous food. The arts and crafts fair at the event center has a lot of holiday merchandise and draws crafters from all over the state. The concert was added about eight years ago when the town built the big event center. It has a huge multi-use area with bleachers that we use for different festivals and concerts during the year."

"For all the festivals that you keep track of on your festival calendar."

She grinned. "The very one."

Chase was sure a good listener to remember

that tiny detail about her. She kind of liked that he remembered that.

"I saw a write up on it in the town newspaper. Saw that Brooks Gallery was a sponsor. At the time I didn't know that *you* were the Brooks Gallery."

"That would be me. Well, my parents started the gallery. Mom loved traveling around to find art to display along with finding a lot of local talent. When she and my father...Well, they were in an accident. They passed away about five years ago."

"I'm so sorry, Sophie."

She looked down at her hands, studying the silver ring encircling her finger, steadying herself. It still hit her at odd moments after all these years, and she had to fight back the tears. She finally looked back up at him. "Well, I took over the gallery after that. I couldn't let all their hard work just die with them."

"It must have been hard to lose both of them at once."

"It was the——" She stopped and took a sip of her drink. "It was the worst time of my life." She took another sip and used the straw to swirl the ice in her drink. "But, I got past it. We always do, don't we? We don't have any choice but to get through what life throws our way."

"No, we don't have any other choice." Chase's eyes were filled with sympathy.

She twisted the ring on her finger. "Luckily Melissa had been working for my mother for years. She knew so much and was so helpful while I was trying to sort everything out."

"The woman with the blonde hair I saw talking to some customers?"

"Yep, that's Melissa. I don't know what I'd do without her."

She took a deep breath. "Anyway, I was a teacher before that. Taught music at the high school. I loved it. Loved teaching the kids. But I left that job to take over the gallery and I've been there ever since."

"That's quite a change from music teacher to gallery owner. Do you enjoy running it?"

Tough question. She did love the gallery. It was part of her parents. It made her feel close to them. But did she enjoying running it?

Well, it wasn't like she had a choice. She would never let her parents' dream die. She looked at Chase. "Sure, I like running it. It's..." She shrugged. "It's what I do."

She looked at him, wondering how to

broach talking about what he did. It's not like she could ask him. Because she knew what he did. It was obvious that Gloria knew who he was even though she hadn't come right out and said anything. He was a famous country singer.

Okay, just lead with that.

"And you're a country singer."

He looked a bit surprised. "You knew? You never said anything."

"Didn't take me long to figure it out. You looked familiar when you showed up at Nora's. You looked a bit different in person than in the photos I've seen of you. You have longer hair now." She grinned at him. "And I'm used to seeing you with your cowboy hat."

"My manager, Sam, insists I wear that hat in all my publicity photos."

"You rock that hat." She grinned again.

He laughed. "Thanks."

"So you're singing solo now?"

CHAPTER 9

A nd there it was. The question he hated.

"I... ah, yes. I'm a solo act now."
Now that Kimberly had gone out on her own.
Gone out on her own and become famous in
her own right.

Not that he begrudged her that.

Well, he did a bit.

Okay, a lot.

She'd taken some of the best songs he'd
written and recorded them herself, and off she'd
rocketed to stardom.

"Do you have an album of your own
solo work?"

"Yes, I do. And about a handful of people
own it."

"I'm sure it takes some time to branch out

on your own." There was a warmth to her gaze and she gave him a soft, encouraging smile.

Time. It had been two long years and he was still struggling. At first, Sam had been able to get him some fairly decent gigs. He'd even got the recording contract for his solo album. But another contract hadn't followed after the dismal response to his first one.

Maybe he wasn't cut out to be a solo act.

He just wasn't sure he was ready to face that fact just yet.

"Did you see that Jackson Dillion is performing at the concert at the end of the Art Weekend?" Sophie continued on, unaware of the turmoil of his thoughts.

He brought himself back to the subject at hand. "I did. Jackson's a great kid. Up and coming. He's a great performer, too. The audience loves him."

"We were lucky to get him."

"I'm sure he'll draw a large crowd for you."

Probably larger than the last crowd that had come out to see his performance. The crowd that had left disappointed...

Their food arrived and saved him from further discussion of his career, or lack thereof.

THEY WALKED out into the chilly night air after what he'd considered one of the best Mexican dinners he'd ever had. Maybe the food. Maybe the company. But he'd had a really good time.

He looked up at the night sky. "Hey, look. It's snowing."

Sophie tilted her face up. "A bit."

The flakes of snow danced around on the breeze, not accumulating much on the sidewalk except for a few sweeps of white near the buildings.

"River walk again or down Main Street?" She looked at him.

"The river walk was nice." He knew he didn't really answer her question, but he was kind of lost in her eyes as the lamplight illuminated her face.

"River walk it is then. I do love walking along the river. It's so soothing. Almost like it's singing its own song, oblivious to whoever hears it." She flashed him a tentative grin. "That sounds a bit silly, doesn't it?"

"Not at all. I feel that way about the wind sometimes. Like it's singing its own song."

"Ah, so you know what I mean." She started down the street.

He wanted to take her hand in his. Which was ridiculous. It was their first date.

With a jolt of surprise, he realized he didn't want it to be their last one. He shoved his hands in his pockets and walked by her side. They bumped shoulders once as they ambled down the sidewalk at a leisurely pace. He was fine with the slow pace. He wasn't ready for the night to be over.

They crossed over to the river walk and strolled down the path, in and out of the light of the lamps scattered along the pathway. She rubbed her arms as they walked along.

"You cold?"

"Just a bit."

"Here." He draped his arm around her shoulder and pulled her against his side. "I'm always running hot." And for once, he was grateful for his hot metabolism.

They continued on down the path, and he tried to ignore how great she felt against his side. Then he quit trying to ignore it and relished it. They walked in sync, in perfect step along the sidewalk. This pathway could go on forever as far as he was concerned.

"Here we are." Sophie stopped by an unmarked doorway in the back of a building.

He realized it must be the gallery. But he still wasn't ready for the evening to be over.

Ask me in. Ask me in. He sent his thoughts winging through the air.

"Would you like to come up for a little while?"

Well, that worked. "Yes, I'd like that."

She opened the door, and he followed her upstairs. She flipped a switch as they entered the loft, low lights came on over the bookcase in the corner, and some lights over the cabinets in the kitchen area glowed and bounced off the ceiling. "I don't like to flood the room with lights at night."

He thought the loft looked enchanting in the low light. Or maybe it was the company.

She slipped out of her jacket before he could help her and hung it on a hook by the door. He draped his jacket beside hers.

"We could sit by the window. I like to sit there and look out over the river."

"Sounds good to me." He followed her over to the window and sank onto the chair next to her. She tugged off her boots, letting them clatter to the floor, and stretched out her long legs.

He pulled his gaze from her legs to the window. "You've got a great view here. It's very peaceful looking out over the water."

"It is. When I took over the gallery, I converted the upstairs into this apartment for me. It just seemed convenient."

"Your parents didn't live here?"

"No, they had a house a little ways out from town. Dad liked his space. Their home is... was... actually, it's on Lone Elk lake, near Nora's lodge. I haven't decided what I'm going to do with it yet. It just sits there." She couldn't bear to live there but couldn't bear to sell it either. So it just sat there. Jason checked on it weekly for her, and she occasionally went there herself but usually left feeling more alone than ever.

"So you and Beth have been friends for a while?"

"Since we were young girls."

He wondered what it would be like to have a friend like that. One who'd known you forever. He didn't even have what most people would consider a best friend. Well, he had Sam, but that was only from the last few years. His father had constantly moved around with his job, and they'd lived in a dozen cities by the time he was twenty and he'd moved to Nashville to try and make it in the music industry. Moving around like that wasn't really conducive to making lifelong friends, or any friends for that matter.

"Beth really helped me after my parents' accident. And Nora always makes sure to invite me over for family dinners. Jason is almost like a brother to me. They're… well, they are almost family to me." She looked at him. "Do you have family?"

He paused for a moment, deciding how to answer. "Just my father." He had to think for a moment where his dad lived now. He'd just moved for yet another job. "Oh, he's in Salt Lake City."

"Do you see him much?"

"No, not much." He frowned trying to remember the last time he'd seen his father. A couple of years? No, more. He'd seen his father after a concert he and Kimberly had in some town. Oh, San Francisco. They'd gone out to eat with his dad.

"And your mom?"

"She's gone."

Which most people assumed he meant dead,

but he really meant gone. She'd disappeared when he was ten, and he'd never heard from her again. She'd left him a letter with a whole list of reasons of why she needed to go.

He hadn't been reason enough to make her stay.

But he never got into that with people. He stood by his cryptic *she's gone* answer.

"I'm sorry." Sophie reached over and touched his hand.

He was sorry his mom was gone, too, so he let the half-truth dissolve into space as he stared down at Sophie's hand covering his.

Her hand was a feather-soft blanket of connection, one he didn't want to break. He slowly flipped his hand over and held hers.

She turned to look out the window, and he watched her. She looked lost in thought and he didn't want to disturb her. Maybe she was thinking about her own mother. She probably had years of wonderful memories with her mom. Something he didn't have with his. Well, he had some good memories from before, back when he was very young. But they'd ended abruptly.

She turned to look at him after a bit and smiled. "I had a good time tonight."

"I did, too."

Her phone rang and she scooped it off the table beside her chair. "It's Beth. I'll call her back later."

They sat quietly for a few more minutes, but the cheerful ring of the phone had shattered the intimacy of the moment. Sophie looked at her watch. "Well, I better be turning in soon. Long day at the gallery tomorrow. I still have so much to do to get ready for the show."

He took his clue and stood. "I should go." He reached a hand down and helped her to her feet. He wanted to continue to hold her hand in his, but he reluctantly let her go. She walked him to the door and stood while he slipped on his jacket, then walked down the stairs with him to the back door. She started to open the door and he reached out to stop her. "I was wondering." He wet his lips. "I was wondering if you'd like to come over to my place at the lodge tomorrow night. I could cook. I make a mean pot of chili. It's the only thing I make, but I promise it's really good."

He wasn't certain what she would say. He could see the indecision flit across her eyes. "I'm pretty busy with the show."

His hopes took a dive.

"But, you know what? I do have to eat. Yes, I'll come over. Can we make it about seven?"

"That would be great. Want me to come pick you up?"

"No, that's okay. I'll drive over."

"Well, I'll see you tomorrow, then." She'd said yes, and he was once again ridiculously happy about that.

"Tomorrow." She opened the door and he slipped outside.

"Good night, Sophie."

"Night, Chase."

He carried the silken tones of her voice with him as he headed to his car. The flakes of snow swirled around him, doing a happy dance right along with him.

CHAPTER 10

"**Y**ou were supposed to call me last night."
Beth's accusing voice came through the
cell phone.

Sophie poured a cup of coffee and walked
over to the window in the loft. "I know, but it
was late when Chase left. I didn't want to
wake you."

"I did crash early. Right after I tried to call
you. I was exhausted."

"See, I did the right thing by not calling
last night."

"So talk to me now."

"I had a good time."

"Just good?"

"No, it was really nice. He's nice. I was kind

of nervous at first, but then we got to talking and… well, it was nice."

"Nice. That word. That's all I'm going to get?"

"He asked me over for dinner tonight."

"Well, that sounds promising."

"He's going to cook chili."

"Two nights in a row with dates."

"I guess you can call them dates." She wondered if Chase thought of them as dates.

"Tonight you should wear that green sweater I gave you last Christmas."

She laughed. "You could just come over and lay out my clothes every morning."

"Just trying to help."

Sophie wandered over to the flowers on the table and adjust them in the vase. "Oh, and he brought me flowers."

"See, I knew I liked the guy."

"Hey, guess who stopped by the table last night? Gloria."

"Ugh."

"No kidding. She managed to slam me, your mother, the lodge, and the town of Sweet River Falls, all within minutes."

"She is one woman who I just can't seem to like. Not even a tiny little bit."

"She makes me crazy. I thought she'd never leave. She gave me the what-in-the-world-is-he-doing-with-you look."

"Don't pay any attention to Gloria. She's an unhappy person who likes to think she's better than everyone else. We should feel sorry for her."

"If you say so. But it would take a lot of effort for me to get to that point."

"Yeah, me, too. Well, I've got to run or I'll be late for school. Have fun tonight."

Sophie set her phone on the table and leaned against the wall beside the window. She stared down at the light covering of snow on the river walk. A lone set of footsteps broke the blanket of white.

She crossed over to the chair where Chase had sat last night and ran her hand along the arm of the chair where his hand had been. She shook her head. What was she doing? And why, of all the men in the world, was she beginning to… What would she even call it? Beginning to be *interested* in Chase Green?

That was not the smartest thing she'd ever done.

～

SOPHIE CLIMBED the steps to Rustic Haven cabin. She smiled when she saw the word rustic carved into the wooden sign by the front door. Gloria would have felt that she'd proven her point about the lodge.

She reached out to knock, but the door swung open before her knuckles reached the wood. Chase stood in the doorway in jeans and a black flannel shirt. His broad shoulders tapered down to his lean waist, where a large silver buckle adorned his leather belt. Well-worn cowboy boots peeked out from the legs of his jeans. He flashed her his famous smile. He looked every bit the country music star.

What was she doing?

"Come in."

She crossed into the cabin and he closed the door behind her. She looked around the cabin. Beth had said her mom and Jason had updated it. It looked more charming to her than *rustic*.

Ugh, Gloria needed to get out of her head.

"I've got the chili going." He reached out to help her take off her coat.

"It smells great." The tangy aroma of it filtered through the room.

"I ran into Nora and told her you were coming to dinner. She sent over fresh homemade bread and some pieces of pie from the dining room for dessert. I think she doubted my cooking ability." He grinned at her.

She looked over at the fire crackling in the fireplace. A comfortable sofa was placed across from it. She did miss having a fireplace. She walked over and stretched her hands out to the heat.

"I've got red wine. Would you like a glass?"

"Yes, please."

She settled onto the sofa, and Chase sat down beside her and handed her a glass of wine.

"Busy day at the gallery?"

"It was. And I was still working on things for the Art Weekend. Got a few late sign-ups for tables for the arts and crafts fair at the event center. That always seems to happen. We always have a big raffle drawing with lots of prizes and got a couple more donations for the grand prize. Then we have smaller prizes like coupons for free dinners at some restaurants in town, a free photo shoot from a local photographer, free t-shirt from a gift shop. Things like that."

"You're organizing all of that along with the show at the gallery?"

"I am." She took a sip of the wine. "My mom was one of the people who started the annual Autumn Art Weekend. I feel responsible for helping with it. To keep it going."

"Sounds like you took over a lot of responsibilities from your parents."

She bristled a bit at his comment. "Well, I had to. I couldn't let the gallery just close. And the Art Weekend was important to Mom. Her vision of sharing all kinds of art with the town and the tourists that come here."

Besides, she owed them this. Owed them this and so much more since their accident had been *all her fault.*

CHAPTER 11

He could immediately see that his remark had struck a nerve with her. "Well, I'm sure your parents would be proud of you."

She seemed to withdraw inside herself as she stared into the fire. He wasn't sure what he'd said that upset her, but the set of her jaw and the look in her eyes clearly showed she was troubled, or unsettled, or maybe even a bit mad at him.

"Sophie, did I say something wrong? I'm not very good at this." What did he know about women or dating or relationships with anyone for that matter?

She turned to him. "No, it's nothing you said. Well, it is, but——" She set her drink on the end table. "I feel like I owe them so much. They were wonderful parents. I want their legacy to live on."

He felt like there was more to her story, but he wasn't about to press her. Time to change the subject.

She must have agreed with him because she got up from the sofa and walked over to where his guitar sat in the corner. "Would you play something for me?"

That he could do. That was familiar. Singing was easier than talking. Well, usually it was. "Sure." He got up and grabbed his guitar. They both settled down on the sofa again as he tuned the strings.

"Got a favorite you want me to sing?"

"You choose."

He launched into one of his favorites about finding forever love. Not that he believed that really happened to people, but the song had a catchy melody to it. She was a great audience and smiled as he finished the song.

"Do another one."

He sang another one as she requested. As he finished that one, he looked at her, remembering the silken tones of her voice as she'd sung to

Trevor and Connor. "How about you do one with me?"

Her eyes widened. "Me?"

"Of course. You have a beautiful voice. How about we sing Road to Forgiveness? Do you know that one?"

"I do."

He strummed a few chords and started into the song. Sophie joined in with her warm, clear tones and harmonized on the refrain. Their voices entwined, and the magnetism of their blended tones launched him into a parallel world. One where his troubles didn't exist. One where he could believe in his songs and his voice again.

The song ended, and their voices faded into the still air. The fireplace crackled and still, he said nothing.

He finally cleared his throat. "That was really nice."

Sophie blushed. "Thank you."

He set the guitar down. He wasn't sure he was ready for another duet. Not after trying for two years to be a solo act. Not even when he felt some kind of magic with their tangled voices. He shoved the thought aside and stood abruptly. "I should check on dinner." He escaped to the kitchen and puttered around, taking up bowls of chili and slices of Nora's homemade bread, totally ignoring the faint tones of the song he swore he could still hear in the cabin. Which was silly.

He set the food on the table. "It's ready."

Sophie got up from the sofa and came over to sit at the table. The rosy blush had faded somewhat from her cheeks. She slipped into her seat. "It looks delicious."

"It's kind of hot. Spicy hot, I mean. Hope you like it."

He sat across from her and took a spoonful of chili. Steam rose from the spoon and he blew on it. "I guess it's hot temperature-wise, too."

He watched while she took a spoonful. She pursed her lips, blew on it, then tasted it. "Oh, it's wonderful."

"Glad you like it." He was ridiculously pleased that she liked it. He realized she often made him ridiculously pleased… and that was… *ridiculous*, wasn't it?

THEY SAT on the couch again after dinner. This time Chase didn't pick up the guitar to sing to her. Or have her sing with him. She couldn't put her finger on it, but something had changed with him as she'd sung with him. Maybe he was sorry he'd asked her. He was used to singing with professional singers, even though she thought they'd sounded nice together.

"So have you decided how long you're staying?" Sophie leaned back on the sofa, resting against its comfortable overstuffed pillows.

"I'm not sure." He smiled at her. "I have to admit, I'm kind of curious about the Autumn Arts Weekend. I'm thinking I might possibly stay until it's over. I talked to Nora and she said she had room for me to stay here."

"Well, I'm prejudiced, but I think the weekend is wonderful and lots of fun."

"I guess that settles it, then. I'll stay."

A strange feeling of relief and happiness rolled over her. She was pleased he was staying. She wanted him to come to the show at the gallery and see the results of all her hard work with the festival.

Though, why she cared, she wasn't sure.

"Well, if I'm staying, and you're in charge of so much, why don't you let me help you?"

She looked at him in surprise. "You want to help?"

"Sure."

She wasn't about to turn down any help for the weekend. Her to-do list was miles long, and she'd already been worrying about how she was going to get so much done in so little time.

"Well, okay... I can use all the help I can get."

"How about I come by the gallery in the morning, and you can put me to work. There, or anywhere you need help."

"Perfect." They sat on the sofa in awkward silence. He'd offered to run errands for her and she didn't even know how to even deal with that offer. Except to accept it, of course. She couldn't quite imagine herself putting Chase Green to work running errands for her, but she was going to have to get over that. There still was tons of work to do.

Speaking of so much to do... She stood. "I really should go now. Thanks for having me."

Chase stood and walked her to the door. "I'm glad you came."

"See you tomorrow."

"Tomorrow." She headed out into the cold night air and hurried to her car. He was still standing in the doorway, outlined by the warm interior lights of the cabin, as she pulled away.

From her second date with Chase Green. The country singer who was going to help her with the Art Weekend.

She shook her head. How in the world had she gotten to this point?

CHAPTER 12

The next morning Sophie rushed around the loft, hoping to get down to the gallery early. She'd spent last night after she got home from Chase's going over her to-do list of things for the weekend. She'd made up a separate list of things Chase could do for her. Picking up flyers from the printer, moving things around in the gallery to get ready to display Hunt's work, confirming with the food trucks to make sure they would be here and assigning them their parking spots. And so many other little details that needed to be done.

Her phone rang and she snatched it off the counter.

"How did last night's date with Chase go?"

"Morning, Beth." She smiled. "I had a good

time. And guess what. He offered to help me with the Art Weekend."

"So, he's staying for a while?"

"He says he wants to stay and see the Art Weekend." She looked around for her shoes. Where had she kicked them off?

"So, since you're my best friend and it seems like he wants to spend time with you, I did some, um… searching on him last night."

"You what?"

"I looked him up on the internet."

Sophie laughed. "Of course you did."

"So, you know that Kimberly person split off from him a couple of years ago?"

"Yes, I knew that."

"Well, he's been doing some solo work since then."

"He said he has a solo album."

"It looks like it didn't sell very well."

"That's what he told me." So far Beth hadn't told her anything she didn't know. And anyway, wasn't it creepy to look someone up on the internet? Even when they were semi-famous. Although she supposed people looked him up online all the time. But it's different when you're… not dating exactly, but… what where they doing?

"So, he had a concert about a month or so ago in Albuquerque and it appears he froze or something. He'd started his first song, then he stopped. Then he just walked off stage and it was cancelled. He had another concert scheduled in Dallas right after that, and he cancelled and they refunded everyone's tickets. Hasn't had one since."

"Maybe he lost his voice or something?"

"Maybe. There's speculation that... well... who knows."

"So maybe that's why he's taking this vacation. Resting his voice." Though his voice sounded just fine last night.

"You're probably right."

"Hey, I've got to go. Got to get down to the gallery."

"Yes, my class should start showing up any minute now, too. I'll talk to you soon."

Sophie set the phone down and turned around and glared at her loft. *Where were those shoes?* She finally saw them peeking out from under the sofa. She hurried over, grabbed them, and slipped them on her feet.

One last look around the loft to make sure the coffee maker was off. She flipped off the lights.

She stood there staring at the loft for a moment, wondering if there was more to the story about Chase and his cancelled concerts. Well, it wasn't really her business, was it? She was just glad that whatever had made him take a break had caused him to come to Sweet River Falls and offer to help her with the Art Weekend. She walked out the door and hurried downstairs to the gallery.

"Miss Brooks?"

A tall man with thick brown hair and a quick smile approached her. It was Hunt, she recognized him from his photo from his website. He looked younger than she'd imagined, though, maybe about her same age. "Mr. Robichaux, it's so good to meet you."

"Call me, Hunt, please. And this is my wife, Keely." A slender woman stood at his side, looking around the gallery with what Sophie hoped was a look of approval.

"Well, Hunt and Keely, I'm very glad to see you. I can't thank you enough for agreeing to do the show."

"I was glad to. And we turned it into a nice

road trip and little vacation." Hunt smiled at Keely and squeezed her hand. "I got us a room at the Pine View B&B. Thanks for the suggestion."

"I usually suggest my friend Nora's lodge, but she's all booked for the weekend."

"The B&B is lovely. We stopped by and dropped off our things ," Keely said.

"I'm glad you like it. Lucy and Ron who run it are a great couple. You'll love Lucy's breakfasts. She's famous for them."

"Your gallery is very nice." Keely looked around the space. "What a great mix of art you have."

"Thank you." Sophie glanced around. She was surprised when people complimented the gallery. She often felt she was falling so short of all her parents had done with it.

"I've got some framed prints in my car I thought you could look through and decide which we'd use. I brought a few canvas wrap photos, too."

"I'd love to see them."

"I'll be right back." Hunt disappeared and came back soon with his arms laden with framed prints. "I've got another load, too."

"Let's go back to my office and we'll look

through them." Sophie led Hunt and Keely to her office. Hunt went and got another two armfuls of his work, and they leaned them against the walls of her office.

She stared at the pieces and slowly began choosing some of them. She came up with two themes. One was his river shots, and one was a series of photos of lone trees.

"I think we could do these two sets, what do you think?"

"You've got a good eye for putting photos together." Hunt nodded. "I think those work well together."

"I have one wall that we'll use for the river photos, and then some standalone displays that we'll use for the trees." Sophie looked at the photos. "I don't suppose you have one more river photo? I could use an odd number of them."

"I'm planning on going on a photo shoot tomorrow. I'll see what I can get. I can get it printed and sent back by two-day shipping. It would be here in plenty of time."

"That would be wonderful."

"So what's the schedule for the Art Weekend?" Keely asked.

"The opening for the show will be Friday

night. That's when people will be expecting to meet Hunt. Then any time he can be around on Saturday will be great. People love to meet the actual artist when they come in to see the work. Saturday night there's a concert at the event center. I can get you tickets if you'd like to go."

"Thank you. We'd love to go." Keely rose from her chair.

Hunt gathered up the photos they hadn't chosen for the show. "I'll drop by the last photo in a few days."

"I look forward to it."

Hunt and Keely left, hand in hand. She hadn't missed the special looks and smiles between them. They were obviously very much in love, and she took an immediate liking to them. She had a good feeling about this showing. Hunt's work was marvelous. Maybe things were going to start going a bit more smoothly for the Art Weekend after all.

CHASE ENJOYED WORKING with Sophie over the next week. He ran errands for her. He helped her hang Hunt Robichaux's work at the gallery. He made phone calls and even convinced her to go out to eat with him again. Twice.

He could see that with his help, Sophie was beginning to relax a bit about all the responsibility she had for the Art Weekend. He'd laughed at her four-page to-do list when he'd seen it, but most of the items were now checked off.

Sophie walked into her office where he was sorting out table placards for the craft show.

"I think things are finally getting wrapped up for the weekend." She set down her ever-present to-do list.

"I'm setting the tables up for the craft fair tomorrow morning. Then I'll help check people in and give them their table assignments on Saturday."

"You've been such a big help."

"I've enjoyed it." He really had. The people in the town were friendly and helpful, and he'd thoroughly enjoyed himself.

"I don't know how I'll ever repay you."

"How about dinner at Antonio's again tonight?" He flashed her a teasing, please-please-pretty-please smile.

She laughed. "How can I refuse?"

"I don't think you can." He nodded with mock sobriety.

"I have to stay until closing tonight, so it will have to be a late dinner. I'll close about eight."

"Then we'll eat late." He was agreeable to any time she picked. As long as she agreed to go out with him again.

Her phone rang and she grabbed it out of her pocket. "Hello?"

He watched while a frown crossed her face, then she reached back and pulled her hair back with one hand, letting it drop slowly back to her shoulders. "I see. No, I understand. I hope he recovers quickly."

She pulled the phone away from her face and clicked it off.

"What is it?" He didn't like the look on her face.

"That was Jackson Dillion's agent."

"And?"

"Jackson was in a car accident. He's in the hospital."

"Is he okay?"

"He will be. But he's not going to make it here for the concert." She let out a long sigh. "I swear this Art Weekend is fighting me every step of the way this year. Everything keeps falling apart. We're almost sold out for the concert. I don't know how my mother ever managed all this and kept things running smoothly. I'm an absolute failure at this."

"No, you're not."

"I have a sold-out benefit concert with no main performer."

"I could do the concert." His words surprised him as much as they did Sophie. He couldn't believe he'd offered, but he couldn't bear to see the look of disappointment on her face.

But he was pretty sure he wasn't ready yet. He didn't even know if he *could* do it.

But he had to.

For Sophie.

"I don't know what to say..." Sophie's eyes were filled with gratitude.

"Say yes."

"Yes. Yes, yes, yes." Sophie twirled around in the office. "This is fabulous. I'm going to do up new flyers right now. Chase Green is going to do a concert for the Autumn Art Weekend." She twirled again.

He grinned at her. He'd do anything to see that smile on her face.

Now, he just hoped he wouldn't disappoint

her…

~

Sophie went back out into the gallery and Chase continued to work on tying up loose ends for the arts and crafts fair portion of the Art Weekend.

His phone rang and he glanced at the caller ID. Sam. He was tempted to let it go to voicemail, but he answered it with a sigh. "Hello."

"Just calling to check in with you." Sam's voice sounded tentative.

Chase laughed. "What you mean is you're trying to figure out if I'm back in Nashville or still away on my forced vacation."

"Okay, maybe," Sam said reluctantly.

"I'm still away. In Colorado."

"Really?"

"Yep. I'm actually having a really good time."

"Well, I have a bit of other news…"

"What?" Chase asked suspiciously.

"Well, we might have a bit of a problem with your next gig. They're getting cold feet after your… well, your problem with your last concerts. They're thinking of cancelling or at least getting another performer to split the stage with you. You haven't been on stage since that… mishap. They're just a bit gun-shy."

"Tell them not to worry. I'm actually doing a benefit concert this weekend. Taking over for Jackson Dillion."

"You are? Without telling me about it?"

"I'm telling you now."

"I heard about Jackson's accident. That's too bad. But where's the concert?"

"It's in Sweet River Falls, Colorado."

"Never heard of it. But I don't care. I'm really glad you're getting back on stage."

"Well, they're having an Art Weekend and the concert is scheduled in conjunction with it. I offered when Jackson had to cancel."

"Well, that's good news. I'll have to put out some publicity for it."

"It's not that big of a deal. It's just a concert at a small-town festival."

"Well, it will be good to see… well, I'm sure when you're a smashing success at the concert that it will allay the fears of the sponsor of your next concert."

He only hoped it *did* allay their fears and he didn't make things worse…

CHAPTER 13

Beth glanced at her watch. She needed to hurry up and get to the lodge. It was getting late. Her mother had picked the boys up from school and fed them dinner. Jason had offered to help them with their homework. She'd had a town council meeting she wanted to attend. She couldn't miss those meetings while she was running for mayor. But the meeting had run late, and now it would be past the boys' bedtime by the time she picked them up and got them home.

She had to figure out a way to juggle all this so it didn't affect the boys so much. She gathered her things and hurried out the door, her mind full of thoughts about the meeting.

The council had talked about rezoning an area outside of town, but Old Man Dobbs had been quiet about his plans to sell his property on Lone Elk Lake. He was probably waiting for when he hoped James Weaver would win the mayor election. Then he'd have more support for rezoning the area around his property.

But that wasn't going to happen. She was going to win this mayoral race and do everything in her power to save the peacefulness of the lake. Zoning changes there could ruin her mother's business at the lodge, not to mention ruin the tranquility of the lake.

She hurried out to her car and drove to the lodge. The welcoming aroma of freshly baked bread and some kind of delicious smelling stew reminded her she hadn't had any dinner.

Her mother greeted her as she entered. "There you are. It's getting kind of late."

"I know. The meeting ran long." She turned and walked into the family room. "Boys, get your things gathered up. We've got to go. It's getting late."

"Mom, you want to see the paper I wrote? Uncle Jason helped me with it. It's on hiking trails around the town. We had to write about something having to do with Sweet River Falls." Connor looked up from the table where he sat with Jason.

"Maybe later, honey. We have to leave." She looked at her watch again. It was going to be more than an hour past their bedtime when she finally got them settled in at home.

Connor jumped up from the table with a scowl plastered on his face. "You never have time for us anymore."

Beth froze, unsure if it was his words or the look on his face that startled her more.

"We're at Grams more than we're at home. You haven't had dinner with us in forever."

"You didn't have time to read to me last night," Trevor added.

"Maybe we should just come live with Grams. *She* has time for us. So does Uncle Jason." Connor turned his back on her and grabbed his backpack.

"Connor, sweetheart. I..." But what could she say to him? He was right. Her mother had been taking care of the boys often while she was busy with the mayoral race. And it seemed like Jason spent more time helping them with their homework than she did the last month or so.

Connor was right, she hadn't had dinner with them in days and days.

Her mother looked over at her. There was no reproach in her eyes, but she stood there waiting to see how Beth would handle the situation.

She had to find a way to juggle everything better. She had to.

"Connor, I'm sorry. I've been so busy with everything while I'm running for mayor."

"I don't know why you want to be the stupid mayor anyway," Connor muttered.

Beth walked over and turned him to look at her. "I'll make more time for you two. I promise. And we'll have dinner at home tomorrow night. How about we make some homemade pizzas?"

"Really?" Trevor came to stand beside Connor. "We haven't done that in *forrrr-ev-errr.*"

"Really. Tomorrow night. I promise."

Her brother looked up from the table. She could see the doubt in his eyes. Well, she'd show all of them. She would pull off the perfect family dinner tomorrow night for her and the boys. It would be great. Nothing would get in the way of it.

~

NORA WALKED into Bookish Cafe the next morning, searching for Annie. Her friend waved to her from across the shop. Nora threaded her way across the store. "Hi, got time for coffee?"

"I always have time for you." Annie greeted her with a hug. "What's up?"

"I... I just wanted to talk."

Annie cocked her head to the side. "Okay, then. Coffee and talk."

They both got a cup of coffee and headed upstairs. They settled into two overstuffed chairs in the corner of the loft area. "So, what's up?" Annie leaned back in her chair.

"Well, I'm trying very hard not to meddle in Beth's life, but... oh, how'd I'd love to give her some advice."

"Like what?"

"Like maybe she's taken on too much?"

"You mean with running for mayor, don't you?"

"Yes. I know part of the reason she's doing it is to have a say in Dobbs' trying to push through rezoning of the lake. She thinks it's her responsibility to help me. Well, and she loves the tranquility of the lake as much as I do."

"She's having a hard time juggling it all?"

"Last night Connor kind of let loose on her. The boys miss seeing her. She's just so busy."

"So why don't you talk to her?"

"She's so fiercely independent now. She's tried so hard to prove she can make it on her own ever since Scott left her. I don't ever want to hold her back."

"Sometimes people we love need to tell us to look at what's right there in front of us. We don't always see the forest for the trees."

"I would like to talk to her about it… but it might just make her even more stubborn about how she can handle it all. I don't mind taking care of the boys so much. I enjoy it. But I'm afraid if I talk to her, she might stop asking for my help just to prove she can do everything."

"Wonder where she gets that stubborn streak?" Annie grinned at her.

"No clue." Nora sent a wry smile back to Annie.

"Well, I still think you should at least try to talk to her."

"I'm trying to be the most supportive mother ever." Nora took a sip of her coffee.

"You always are and always have been. But Beth listens to you. You should at least broach the subject."

"Maybe." Nora looked over her cup, not really seeing what was going on around them. Maybe Annie was right. Maybe she should talk to Beth. She was just worried that she might make things worse.

CHAPTER 14

S ophie looked up from her desk to see Chase standing in the doorway.

"Hey, I've been a great helper, haven't I?" He gave her a sly grin.

"You have."

"We've waded through your to-do list like champions."

"That we have." She had to admit she was breathing a bit easier about the Art Weekend.

"So, why don't you take the afternoon off and we'll go for a hike in the mountains? I've been here all this time and haven't made it on one hike yet. Seems a shame, doesn't it?" He tossed her another lopsided grin.

Sophie debated. There was still a lot to do for the Art Weekend, but it would be great to get out in the fresh air, and they were having a wonderfully mild day. The sunshine and fresh air finally won out. Or maybe it was his grin. Who could resist that boyish grin?

"Okay. It's a deal. Melissa can watch the gallery. Give me thirty minutes to wrap things up here and change."

"Annie told me about a hike to Lost Lake."

"That's a good one. We have enough time to do it in an afternoon, and the views are amazing."

"Perfect. Let me run to the lodge and change, too."

"I'll meet you there at the lodge. It's on the way to the trailhead."

"Okay, I'll see you soon."

She watched while he disappeared out the door. She couldn't believe she was taking an afternoon off this close to the Art Weekend.

She couldn't believe she was taking a hike with Chase Green.

She really needed to stop thinking that way about Chase all the time. They'd actually kind of became friends while he'd helped her with the Art Weekend.

Friends with Chase Green.

Stop it.

She got up and hurried upstairs to change.

CHASE OPENED the door to Rustic Haven to see Sophie standing there in hiking boots, jeans, and a bright yellow jacket.

"Come on, I'll drive us." She beckoned to him.

He grabbed his jacket and backpack and headed after her. Before long, they pulled into parking near the trailhead to Lost Lake.

They got out and put on their packs. He hadn't really known what a hiker packed, but he'd put in a water bottle, some snacks, and a pocket knife. Because every hiker carried a pocket knife, right?

Sophie led the way to the trail, and they began their ascent. He considered himself a man in good condition. Well, fairly good condition. But the altitude began to kick his behind when they climbed above tree line. He gasped for breath as he struggled to keep up with her.

She made the ascent look effortless.

She looked back at him and grinned. "How about we take a quick break?"

He gratefully collapsed on a large boulder beside the trail and dug out his water bottle, taking a long swallow.

"The altitude is a killer when you're not used to it." Sophie sat beside him.

He wasn't sure he wanted to waste any oxygen talking to her...

They sat for a few minutes staring off at a fantastic view of the snow-capped mountains in the distance.

"It's one of my favorite views." Sophie nodded toward the mountain peaks.

He finally thought his lungs had gotten enough oxygen that he could answer her. "It is an amazing view."

She turned to him. "You think you're ready to go on? We just need to go over that pass, then we'll drop down into a valley that has the lake."

"Sure, I'm ready." Was he? He hated feeling so out of shape.

They climbed to the top of the pass and he looked down below them. The view almost took his breath away, as if the altitude hadn't already done that. An emerald green lake sparkled in the valley, nestled between the two mountains. At the far end, a waterfall splashed into a stream that fed into the lake.

"Okay, that is an amazing view, too. I've never seen anything like it."

"There's another lake further up."

He looked at her in dismay and she laughed.

"No, we're not going there. It's an all-day hike to get there and back. Come on, let's hike down to Lost Lake."

They picked their way down the rocky terrain until they reached the lakeside. He sat beside her as she took off her backpack. He stretched out on the rock and let the bright sunshine wash over him.

She stretched out beside him and baked in the warmth, too.

He wasn't sure there was ever a more perfect moment. Just resting here with Sophie at his side.

He was actually even beginning to breathe a little better.

She sat up and rustled around in her backpack, leaving him feeling alone as he reached out a hand to where she had just been lying beside him.

"Here, want a peanut butter sandwich?"

"I do." He sat up and reached for it. Suddenly he was famished.

"I always get hungry when I hike. I like a

peanut butter sandwich for some quick protein." She took a bite of her sandwich.

He devoured his, then drank some more of his water. He slipped the empty bottle back into his backpack noticing the unused pocketknife resting in the bottom. He wasn't sure what he was going to drink on the trip down.

She looked over at him and smiled. "I have an extra water bottle for you. Wasn't sure if you'd realize how climbing in this altitude can make you so thirsty. Well, and then the peanut butter."

She handed him another bottle of water and stood. "We should probably head back. Don't want to get caught on the trail after nightfall."

He reluctantly stood up.

"It's just the climb back up to the pass, then it will all be downhill from there."

That suited him just fine. He wished he had more time to stay here and get used to the altitude and get in better shape for more hiking.

After they got over the pass again and started down the path, Sophie started a game she called trail questions.

"What's your favorite color?" She asked him.

"Blue." Which he wasn't sure it was, but

with the brilliant blue sky above him that so reminded him of her sparkling blue eyes, no other color would come to mind.

"Now you ask me a question." She paused on the path and looked at him.

"Okay, what's your favorite color?"

"Yellow, but you can't ask the same question. That's cheating."

He grinned. "Sorry, didn't know all the rules. Okay, did you have any pets growing up?"

"I did. I had a calico cat. Miss Kitty. Loved her so much." She continued down the path that was now wide enough for them to walk side by side. "What's the most interesting place you've ever been?"

"That's easy. Sweet River Falls." He grinned at her. "Sunrise or sunset?"

"Sunrise. Definitely." She bobbed her head in emphasis.

"Really, why?"

"It's the start of a new day. A new chapter. A new beginning." She shrugged. "I don't know. I've always loved them."

He could understand that. Sometimes new beginnings were the best thing. Though sometimes they didn't turn out like planned...

like his supposed new beginning of his solo career.

"What's your favorite drink?"

"I'm pretty sure it's now the margaritas at Antonio's."

She laughed her adorable laugh. The one he loved to make happen.

"What's your guilty pleasure?" He eyed her.

She blushed that lovely rose color that he also loved to make happen. "Donuts. Lots of them. It's embarrassing how many I can eat. Any kind, but simple glazed are my favorite."

"And here I brought you flowers. I should have brought donuts," he teased.

"What's one thing you'd change about your life?"

He wasn't about to tell her the truth on that one. He didn't even admit that to himself. "Well, I wish I'd come to Sweet River Falls sooner."

"I think you're cheating on your answers. They all involved being here."

"Because being here is my favorite of everything."

The path got narrow and he stepped ahead of her onto a rock and reached down his hand for her. She placed her hand in his, and he pulled her forward. The path widened again, but he kept her hand in his, enjoying the connection.

What was his biggest regret? He silently asked himself the question. He regretted not taking a hike with Sophie before this.

CHAPTER 15

The next afternoon Beth bustled around, clearing her desk in her classroom. She had dinner plans with the boys, and she was not going to mess that up. She looked up and saw Mac standing in the doorway.

Torn, she was glad to see him, but she'd promised the boys that just the three of them would have dinner. But it seemed rude not to ask Mac, now that he was here in town. She gave him a weak smile.

He frowned and entered the classroom. Her phone rang and she gave him a just-a-minute sign. "Hello?"

Walter Dobbs's voice came clearly through the phone. And he was annoyed. "We need you over here at city hall."

"What's wrong?"

"There's a mess-up on the permits for the Arts Weekend. You filed them for your friend Sophie Brooks, didn't you?"

Beth frowned. "I did."

"Well, if you can't even fill out the paperwork for permits properly, how do you expect to run the town if you become mayor?"

"What's wrong with the permits?"

"You didn't get all the signatures."

Beth tried to picture the forms she'd filled out for Sophie. The one for the concert at the events center and another one for the crafts festival. "I'm sure I—"

"You need the event center manager's signature on these. I called him so that you didn't ruin the Arts Weekend for the whole town, but for legal reasons we still need the manager's signature."

"I'll come by tomorrow and pick up the form and get his signature."

"The deadline is tonight. If you don't fix it, there'll be no craft show or concert this weekend."

"Okay, I'll be there in a few minutes." She clicked off the phone and looked at her watch. Dobbs could have easily gotten the signature, but of course, he wouldn't think of helping her out.

Anyway, it *was* her fault. She remembered now that she was supposed to run the forms by the events center manager. With all that was going on, she'd let that detail slip by. And Dobbs had oh so clearly pointed out that she couldn't let details slide if she wanted to be mayor.

"You okay?" Mac walked over and gave her a quick kiss.

"I—" She let out a long breath of air. "I'm fine. I just need to go run one quick errand. But I need to get the boys from after-school sports, and then I promised the three of us would make homemade pizza tonight. They're a little upset with me. I haven't been spending much time with them."

"I could pick them up from sports and take them to your house. You could meet us there."

"I—" How could she let him do that for her then not ask him to stay?

"As soon as you get there, I'll leave. Let the three of you have a family dinner."

She sent him a grateful look. Mac always seemed to know what she needed. "I promise I won't be long."

"Go. I'll go get the boys from the gym and take them to your house."

"Thanks, Mac. You're the best." She gave him a hug and slipped on her jacket. "Won't be long, I promise."

"Boys, why don't you hang up your coats? Do you have homework? We could get started on that." Mac followed the boys into Beth's house.

"Mom was going to help us with homework tonight. And she said we'd make pizza." Trevor looked at him, his blue eyes questioning, or maybe accusing.

"She promised she'd be here soon. She just had to run an errand."

"Right." Connor's voice was filled with doubt.

The boys went and hung up their coats. Mac stood there, not sure what to do. It would help Beth out if the boys got some of their homework knocked out, but if she said she'd help them...

"I'm going to my room." Connor marched out of the room and down the hallway.

"We could play a game or something while

we wait for Mom." Trevor looked at him with his clear blue eyes full of hope.

"Sure, how about a card game?"

"We could play go fish."

Mac didn't know how to play that exactly, but he'd figure it out. How hard could it be?

An hour and a half later, he and Trevor were still playing cards, and no sign of Beth. Connor came out of his room. "I'm starving."

"Well, if I knew how to make pizza, we could get it started, but the only kind of pizza I've ever made is throwing a frozen one in the oven."

"It doesn't matter. Mom's not going to get here in time for dinner. I'm just going to make a peanut butter sandwich."

"Why don't you wait for just a little bit more? I'm sure your mom will be here soon."

"No, she won't. She promised she would, but she breaks her promises now." Connor stalked over to the kitchen cabinet and pulled out a jar of peanut butter, banging it down on the counter.

Mac was at a loss. He didn't know anything about raising kids. Didn't know if he should insist that Connor wait for Beth. He looked at his watch. It *was* getting late, and the boy probably was hungry.

"Here, I'll make you a sandwich." Mac stood.

"Will you make me one, too? I'm dying I'm so hungry." Trevor bounced in his chair.

"You got it. Two sandwiches, coming up." He just hoped Beth didn't kill him when she showed up.

He sat with the boys while they ate their sandwiches and some slices of apple. That's all he'd found that he knew how to make.

Just as they were finishing up, Beth rushed through the door. She stopped short when she saw the almost finished meals on the boys' plates. She turned accusing eyes on him.

Okay, then. He'd made the wrong choice.

"I thought we were going to make homemade pizza tonight?" Beth looked at the boys.

Connor looked right back at her. "You weren't here and we were starving."

A guilty look passed over Beth's face. She glanced at her watch. "It's not that late."

"We don't have our homework done either," Trevor said as he reached for another slice of apple.

"I'm going to do my homework alone. In my room." Connor got up, grabbed his backpack, and disappeared down the hallway. His door closed with a resounding thud.

Beth turned to Mac. "It took longer than I thought. The event manager was gone when I got there, and I had to track him down for his signature. Sophie would never forgive me if I messed this up. It's about the only thing I've helped her with this year for the Arts Weekend. I usually help her with a lot of the running of it. I wasn't even on the Arts Committee this year."

She sank into a chair at the table. "I'm sorry Trev."

"It's okay, Mom. I know you're busy."

"Why don't you get your books out and I'll help you with your homework?"

"I should go." Mac stood.

"I'll walk you out." Beth stood, slipped off her coat, and dropped it on the chair.

He followed her to her front door. "I'm sorry, Beth. They were hungry and I wasn't sure what to do."

"No, it's my fault. I was late. I'm sure they were starving." She let out a sigh. "I promised them, and then I didn't make it home in time. I'm letting everyone down."

"Maybe you've taken on too much responsibility."

"Mac, it's all things I *need* to do."

He took a deep breath, cocked his head to the side, and looked directly at her. "Is it?"

When she didn't answer, he quietly slipped out the door.

CHAPTER 16

Sophie looked around the gallery, double checking that everything looked in order. Just one hour until the official opening of the show. Hunt and Keely had promised they'd be here before the start.

She looked up as Chase walked through the front door carrying a large bouquet of flowers. He walked up to her. "These are for you."

"What for?"

"Good luck on the show. Good luck with the whole Art Weekend. Well, just because I know how hard you've worked." He handed the flowers to her.

"Thank you. That is so sweet." She buried her nose in the bouquet and took in a deep breath. "I'm going to put them in a vase and set them on the table with the refreshments."

"Now, what can I do to help?" Chase slipped off his coat.

"You could work the refreshment table? Make sure there are always glasses of champagne. And if we run out of any appetizers, there are more trays to put out back in my office."

"Sure thing, I'm your man."

The words caught her off guard. He wasn't exactly *her man*, but she certainly enjoyed being around him. He'd been a wonderful help to her these last days.

She was going to miss him when he left Sweet River Falls.

With a falling heart, she realized he would leave. And leave soon. Back to his real life in Nashville. She might never even see him again. She'd been so busy the last week that she hadn't even thought about the future. The future that didn't have Chase Green's mesmerizing smile every day.

He walked over to the refreshment table, unaware of the turmoil of her thoughts. Eventually, she'd look back at this time with Chase and wonder if it had even been real.

They'd gone out to dinner, he'd cooked for her, he'd sung for her and run a million little errands for her to get the Art Weekend all set up. They'd talked about anything and everything as they worked. She felt like she'd gotten to know the real Chase Green, not the country singer persona the world knew.

And she liked the real Chase Green. She liked him a lot.

CHASE LOOKED across the crowded gallery at Sophie chatting with Hunt and some customer, looking at a large print of a lone pine tree on a mountainside. It was one of his personal favorites of Hunt's work.

Sophie looked over at him and smiled. He gave a little wave back at her, then turned to pour another half dozen glasses of champagne. She must be so proud. The show was a great success. Many of the art pieces had sold signs on them already. Hunt had a series of the river photos on display, and they were taking orders for signed and numbered prints of them to be shipped to the customers in time for Christmas.

Sophie had thought of everything. He was

impressed by her hard work and efficiency, not to mention her friendly, easy-going manner with the constant stream of people coming into the gallery.

He'd really enjoyed his time here in Sweet River Falls. It had been a welcome break from the stress of life in Nashville. A way to escape the constant reminder of his failures. The solo album and his cancelled concerts.

He still hadn't gotten over the shock of what he thought he'd seen at the concert in Albuquerque. He'd literally been dumbstruck. So much so that he'd walked off the stage. So unprofessional, and he regretted it, but he couldn't change it now.

And now he doubted what he'd seen anyway. It didn't make any sense.

He shook his head and turned to a customer at the table. "Here you go." He handed her a glass of champagne. She looked vaguely familiar.

"I'm Gloria Edmunds. You met me at Antonio's."

"That's right. Gloria, good to see you."

"I thought I'd drop by and see what Sophie had done with the show here at her little gallery."

Somehow Gloria's words sounded like she was belittling Sophie. Or maybe he'd just become overly protective of her.

"Sophie's done a fabulous job. The place has been packed all evening. She's done a great job planning the whole weekend, actually."

Gloria gave him a doubtful look. "I guess. It's a nice little weekend, I suppose, but it's not like Sweet River Falls is an art mecca or anything. I guess people will come to about any kind of festival though."

He gritted his teeth and forced a smile. "I'm sure the weekend will be a great success for the town."

"I heard you're going to sing at the concert tomorrow."

"I am." He hoped he was. *You know, if he could get over his absolute fear of seeing a mirage again.*

It had to have been a mirage. Not real.

"Well, I'll be there. I couldn't get very good seats. I'm pretty far in the back. Disappointing, but I'll be there."

He nodded.

She downed her glass of champagne and headed out the door without so much as a brief look at any of the artwork.

~

SOPHIE CLOSED and locked the door as Hunt and Keely left the shop. She turned to Chase and grinned. "That went well."

"I'll say. The gallery was packed all evening."

"We did such a great business. Best turnout I've ever had for a show. Almost all of Hunt's work is sold already. He's going to bring in a few more photos for tomorrow. His work is just so emotional. I think the customers felt a real connection to it."

"I'm glad it all worked out so well for you."

"Now, I hope the craft fair tomorrow goes well, too. I heard that every room in town is sold out, along with most of the rooms in Mountain Grove."

He looked at her blankly.

"Oh, Mountain Grove is a town about twenty minutes away. Closest town to Sweet River Falls. Mac—you met him at Nora's—he lives in Mountain Grove. Has a tavern there."

"Well, you obviously did a great job advertising the weekend."

"It sure helped that the weather cooperated,

A SONG TO REMEMBER

too. We've had snow on the Art Weekend before. One year it totally got cancelled because of the snow. No one could get to town."

"Then you lucked out." He smiled at her.

"I can't thank you enough for your help with everything. And for offering to sing at the concert tomorrow."

"I'm glad I could help."

"I don't know how I can repay you."

"How about taking two of these glasses of champagne up to your loft and sitting by the window? I could use a bit of a sit down about now."

She picked up the last two glasses of champagne sitting on the table. "Follow me." She turned out the main gallery lights as they headed up the stairs.

Once upstairs, they settled into the chairs by the window. She kicked off her shoes. "Oh, that feels better."

Chase leaned back in his chair and stretched out his long legs. "I guess I should rest while I can. I'm working the craft show in the morning, then I'll be standing on stage tomorrow night."

"Are you sure you don't want me to find someone to take your shift at the craft show?"

"Nope, I'm more than willing to help."

She wanted to ask him when he planned to leave town. Only, she didn't really want to know the answer. Didn't want to think about it.

But she was used to carefully planning out her life. She should ask him so she could plan for…

What *was* she planning for? Disappointment? Loneliness?

With a start, she realized she would miss him. She'd be lonely. He'd slipped into her life in an easy routine. She was used to seeing him every day and having dinner with him most nights. Her life would be so different when he was gone.

She leaned back in her chair and closed her eyes. Nope, she wasn't going to ask him. She was just going to enjoy every last moment she had with him. Then he'd move on and she'd learn to adjust. She always learned to adjust to the curves that life threw her.

CHASE LOOKED over at Sophie leaning back in her chair, her eyes closed. She must be exhausted. She'd done so much to get ready for the gallery show as well as orchestrating most of the Art Weekend.

He was going to miss her when he left town. Miss working with her, miss her smile. Suddenly, he wasn't so anxious to leave and get back to his life in Nashville. He wasn't anxious to leave her loft either.

He wanted nothing more than to sit and look at her, talk to her.

No, that was wrong. He *did* want more.

He wanted to kiss her.

He swallowed. Getting romantically involved with Sophie made absolutely no sense. None. None at all. It was ridiculous.

Yet, there it was. His thought.

He wanted to kiss her.

He leaned toward her and she opened her eyes at the sound of his movement. She smiled at him.

That was all it took. He leaned closer and reached out to touch her face. Her skin was so soft.

Her eyes widened.

He leaned in even more, inches from her, then moved closer to kiss her. Gently. Questioningly.

Her lips kissed back eagerly, and a sigh escaped her.

He pulled back slightly and looked into her eyes. Her cheeks were flushed a lovely rosy pink, and her blue eyes shone with anticipation. He rose to his feet, reaching down to pull her up with him.

He took her in his arms, relishing the feeling of her against him, feeling her heart beat wildly. He tilted her chin up and kissed her again. Then his thoughts tangled, and he wasn't sure how long they stood there kissing in front of her window overlooking the river rushing by below them. It was like they were caught up in its currents.

She finally pulled away and looked directly into his eyes. "I wasn't… well, I wasn't expecting that."

He gave a low laugh. "I wasn't either." He wanted to explain how it didn't make sense and that should be their last kiss. Last kiss ever. Instead, he brushed another quick kiss against her lips. "I should… go."

She nodded without saying a word.

He grabbed his jacket and left, heading down the stairs, careful to lock the back door behind him. He stood beside the river, under the lamplight, and looked up to her window.

She stood softly illuminated in the low light of her apartment. She lifted a hand in a wave. He returned the wave and turned and headed down the river walk. After a few minutes, he realized he'd headed in the wrong direction and headed to the street to go find his car.

CHAPTER 17

The next morning Sophie kept expecting Chase to show up at the gallery, but he didn't. She knew he was working at the craft fair, but she still thought that maybe...

What did she think? He would come by because he'd kissed her? The kisses probably hadn't meant anything to him. How could they? He was leaving. Maybe leaving tomorrow. It was just a kiss. Well, more than one kiss.

She reached up and touched her lips.

Only it wasn't just a kiss to her.

Or maybe it was.

Her thoughts whirled in circles. She should be concentrating on her work, not her relationship with Chase. Which wasn't really even a relationship. They were friends, right? New, just met recently friends, at that.

She carefully straightened a print on the gallery wall though it was probably already straight.

At the sound of someone approaching, she turned around, grateful to see Hunt's friendly face. "Hey, Hunt. The opening went great last night."

"I'll say. You did a great job with it." Hunt smiled at her.

"You drew in a large crowd and they loved talking to you. Many of them recognized some of the places you photographed."

"I had a good time talking to them, too. I really did. You have yourself quite a nice gallery here."

"Thanks. It's really my parents' gallery. Or it was. I mean…" She shoved her hair away from her face. "It's mine. I took it over from them. Anyway, thanks for the compliment." Could she sound anymore lame?

"Keely and I are going to go see the craft fair. She's hoping to do some holiday shopping. I just wanted to check and see if you needed anything from me before we head out."

"No, I'm good."

"We'll stop by late afternoon and see how things are going, then we're headed for the concert tonight. Keely is excited to hear Chase Green."

"I am, too." She *was* excited to hear Chase tonight. And excited to see him…

Hunt left and she went back to work. She turned around when she heard the door open again, hoping it was Chase. Instead, she was greeted by Beth's wide smile. "Hey, Sophie. I just wanted to pop in and see how things were going."

"They're great. Lots of sales. Hunt has really drawn a crowd."

"I bet you've sold a lot of your silver work too."

"I have. I was surprised."

"Sophie, Sophie, Sophie, what am I going to do with you?" Beth hugged her. "Your work is wonderful. You need to believe in yourself."

"I'm just always surprised when it sells so well."

"Speaking of believing in yourself… and how wonderful you are… how are things going with Chase?"

She felt a wide grin spread across her face.

"Ah, ha. I knew it." Beth grinned back triumphantly.

"Things are going well. I feel like I'm beginning to get to know the real Chase. Not the famous singer Chase, but him as a man."

"And you like him, don't you?"

"Sure, I like him."

"I mean, like-like him." Beth peered at her.

"We're just… friends." The heat of a blush crept over her cheeks.

"I see that blush. Spill it."

"Well… he kissed me."

"Told you he liked you."

"I don't know…"

"Seriously, Sophie, I love you dearly, but you've got to start believing in yourself."

CHASE STOOD backstage and paced back and forth. Stagehands hurried around finishing up their jobs. He had tuned his guitar. Tuned it three times. He pulled at the collar of his black shirt. Maybe it was too tight. Maybe he'd made the wrong choice wearing it. Even his most comfortable cowboy boots were nagging his feet.

He ignored them and stalked the length of

the backstage area again, counting his steps, then glanced at his watch. Ten more minutes. An eternity and yet not enough time.

Surely he wouldn't screw up this time. He couldn't. Sophie was depending on him.

He would be fine.

Just fine.

He turned on his heels and stomped back the other direction. Where was Sophie? She'd acted like it was a really big deal to her that he was doing this concert, yet she wasn't even here. She'd left him alone to deal with his anxiety.

Not that she'd known he'd *be* this anxious.

He was fine.

He spun around at the sound of a flurry of activity behind him. Sophie hurried up to him. "There you are. Are you ready to go?"

He forced a smile. "Yep." He was so relieved to see her he had to keep himself from throwing his arms around her and sweeping her up in a hug. He knew she had responsibilities at the gallery, but he just wanted...

What *did* he want? Her presence? Her support? Well, here she was with her sparkling eyes, bubbling enthusiasm, and total faith in him, however displaced that might be.

155

"The center is packed." She peeked out at the crowd.

"I figured people would cancel when they heard that Jackson wasn't performing." He wasn't sure he *wanted* a packed crowd. He reminded himself that this was a smaller venue. He'd done much larger concerts. There was no reason to be nervous.

Sophie turned and looked at him. "Are you kidding me? We sold more tickets since everyone found out that Chase Green himself would be performing." She smiled at him.

He took a deep breath. Yes, he *was* performing tonight.

He would be fine.

Just fine.

How many times could he tell himself that?

The event coordinator went out on stage and introduced him. Sophie smiled encouragingly at him. She hesitated, then leaned up and gave him a quick kiss on his check. "Break a leg."

Was break a leg the proper thing to say to someone performing a concert, or just to an actor?

Well, he was going to be acting. He was going to act like this was no big deal. He was going to act like he was fine. He took a deep breath and headed out on stage.

The crowd cheered, and he lifted a hand in a wave. "Hello, Sweet River Falls."

The crowd answered with an echoing hello.

He turned to the band and nodded. They started into the intro of his first song. He swung his guitar into position and took a few steps toward the front of the stage.

Then it happened. He looked at the front row.

His mirage.

Again.

He vaguely heard the band as they played the intro a second time, waiting for him to join in.

Front and center in the crowd, the mirage was right there.

She was there again.

Sophie frowned as the band played the intro a second time. Chase was just standing there staring out into the audience. A memory of what Beth told her about Chase freezing at his last concert flashed through her mind. Was it happening again? Without taking time to think it through, she walked out on stage.

She crossed through the bright lights and went to stand beside Chase. "You okay?" She mouthed the words.

He just looked at her.

"Chase?" She said his name.

This time he turned his attention to her and actually saw her standing there. She reached out and put her hand on his arm.

He shook his head.

She turned and motioned to the sound guy to cut Chase's microphone. She could hear the crowd getting restless.

"Chase, is everything okay?"

"I can't." He whispered the words.

"Sure you can. It's okay. Look at me."

He turned and looked right into her eyes.

She couldn't believe she was offering this, but she didn't know how else to help him. She licked her lips. "How about we start with a duet? We could do that song you wrote. A Song to Remember."

He nodded at her. Sort of. She was going to take that as a yes. She turned to the sound man and motioned to turn the mic back on and hurried over to grab a mic of her own.

"Well, Chase here has convinced me to sing a duet with him tonight." She smiled and waved to the audience. "Hope you enjoy."

The band started the intro, and she looked right at Chase and nodded. They both started into the words, and Chase's voice strengthened as they got into the first verse. He joined in playing his guitar, and their voices entwined, filling the event center with the clear tones of the song. It was one of her favorites of his, and the throng of concert-goers seemed to love it. The crowd even joined in on the refrain.

The song ended, and the center erupted in applause.

"You good now?"

He nodded.

"Okay, I'll leave you to it." She turned to leave, and he reached for her, the slightest touch on her elbow. She turned to look at him.

"Stay." His eyes pleaded with her.

"You sure?"

"I'm sure."

"Well, let's do this, then." She grinned at him and motioned to the band. They sang another set of songs to deafening applause after they finished each one. Slowly Chase began to

159

relax and smile. He almost seemed like his normal self.

Almost.

There was an edge to him, and he kept looking out at the front section of fans.

"How about we wrap up with Road to Forgiveness?" He played a few chords.

She nodded back at him and waited while the band started up again. Chase started into the first verse of the song, and she joined him on the refrain. She sang the second verse, and he joined in on the refrain again. They both sang the last verse, their voices dancing through the arena, in a haunting, twisting spiral of the final refrain.

Once again the crowd erupted in applause. She couldn't help the grin that spread across her face. Music. She had so missed her music. She'd missed that spark of joy that singing brought to her. She felt most like her authentic self when she was lost in a song. Is this something she could have had, if not for the accident and needing to run the gallery?

This was no time to think about that.

They waved to the crowd, and Chase took her hand firmly in his and led her off stage.

Chase wrapped her in a hug as soon as they

hit the backstage area. "Thank you, Sophie. I couldn't have done it without you."

"What happened out there?" She looked up at him.

He scraped a hand over his face. "I—"

Just then Beth came rushing up to them and threw her arms around her. "Sophie Brooks. Look at you. You were wonderful."

"She was." Chase nodded.

"You two were fabulous together. Soph, I haven't heard you sing like that in forever. I swear you were born to sing."

"Says my unbiased best friend." She grinned at Beth.

More people came up to congratulate them, and Sophie basked in the praise and congratulations. Tonight had been the most thrilling night of her life. She had sung on stage with an honest-to-goodness, famous country star.

And she'd had the time of her life.

But she still was going to find out what happened with Chase. Why he froze. He wasn't going to get away with a non-answer.

THE CROWD FINALLY DIED DOWN, and she and Chase sat alone in the small room that doubled as a dressing room for performers but in reality was just a supply room.

"So are you going to talk to me? Tell me what happened." She reached out and took his hand in hers.

He sat there not speaking, and for a minute she thought he wasn't going to answer her.

He finally leaned forward. "I— I saw her. I mean I think I saw her. I think it was her."

"Who?" A frown wrinkled her forehead. He wasn't making much sense.

"My—" He cleared his throat and looked right at her. "My mother."

His mother was dead. Was he seeing ghosts? "You said she was dead."

"No, I said she was *gone*."

"So she's not dead?" Her head started to spin. He was not making any sense.

"I guess not. I didn't really know for sure. But then I saw her sitting in the front row. Just like I did in Albuquerque. First time I'd seen her in over twenty-five years."

"I don't understand." She still couldn't get over the fact his mother wasn't dead. She was *gone*. That's what he'd told her. She'd assumed he meant dead. And he sure hadn't corrected that assumption.

"My mother left. Left us, my father and I. Disappeared right after Garrett died."

"Who's Garrett?"

"My brother."

Now her head was twirling with thoughts as she tried to sort out all he had told her.

She realized that she didn't know anything about this man sitting in front of her. All her illusions that she'd gotten to know the real Chase Green burst into a million tiny shards of glass.

Who was this man?

CHAPTER 18

Guilt washed over Chase. He'd known Sophie thought his mom was dead, and he'd done nothing to change that or tell her the truth. Now, when the truth came out, he could see the hurt clearly etched on her face.

"I'm sorry, Sophie. It's just always been easier to... to forget it all happened." He dragged his hand through his hair. "It was such a rough time in my life. My brother was my best friend. He was two years older than me and we did everything together. We had this perfect family life. Vacations, family dinners, and lots and lots of laughter. Then Garrett got sick. Cancer. The next few years were all about doctors and hospitals. They were all about

Garrett, as they should have been, but it was like I no longer existed."

He stood up and paced the floor. "I resented the attention he got, which was silly. I mean he got attention because he had *cancer*, for Pete's sake." He mindlessly picked up a flyer about the concert, then set it back down.

She still hadn't said a word, but he could see the pity in her eyes. He didn't want pity. His life had just been what it had been. He'd already dealt with all the pain.

At least he thought he had until he'd seen his mother again.

He swallowed. "Garrett died after two years of fighting the cancer. The day after his funeral, I woke up to find a note on the bed table. Mom said she had to leave. She had all these reasons. She said she loved me but couldn't stay."

"Chase, I'm so sorry."

"Yes, well, it was hard at the time. I kept imagining she'd return. But I never got a phone call, a card, or anything."

"Then you saw her in the audience in Albuquerque?"

"I thought so. But then, after I walked off the stage, well, then I wasn't sure. I thought my mind had been playing tricks. But I full out panicked about my next concert in Dallas and told Sam I'd lost my voice, so we cancelled."

"And you thought you saw her again tonight?"

"I'm sure I did." There was no doubt or mistake this time. He'd seen her. She'd given him a little smile and a wave.

Why, after all this time had she decided to come hear him sing?

A knock at the door drew him out of his thoughts. He didn't want to be interrupted now. He needed time to think. Time to try and explain things to Sophie. Someone knocked again, louder this time.

He stalked over to the door and yanked it open.

"HELLO, CHASE."

There she was. He could no longer trick himself into believing she was a mirage. She was right there in front of him. She looked so much the same, and yet different. Older. Her hair had grayed and no longer floated around her shoulders. She wore it in a short cut with wisps of curls framing her face. Wrinkles etched her face at the sides of her eyes, but her eyes were still the same crystal-clear sky-blue color he remembered.

"May I come in?"

He didn't move. He didn't even know if he was breathing.

Somewhere in the distance of reality, he felt the sudden closeness and warmth of Sophie at his side. He saw Sophie's hand snake out toward…

His *mother*. Only she didn't get to call herself that. She'd abandoned him. A mother didn't abandon their child. All the anger and fury and hurt he'd buried for so many years burst around him, engulfing him in a furor he didn't know how to control.

He stepped back from the door. "No, I don't think you should come in. I have nothing to say to you."

"Chase, please." Her blue eyes implored him.

Well, he hadn't even been given a chance to beg her to stay all those years ago. She hadn't given him that opportunity. Why should he let her in now? Let her into the room, or into his life?

Sophie looked at him, then turned to his mother. "Maybe now isn't a good time."

"I just want to say..." A lone tear trailed down his mother's—no, *the woman's*—face.

It would not move him. Not the look in her eyes, or the tear on her cheek.

"Chase, I'm so sorry. I know that doesn't mean much after all this time. But I am sorry. And I just want you to know I love you. I've always loved you."

She gave him a searching look like she was memorizing all his features. "I'm staying at Pine View B&B for a few days. I'd love it if you'd come see me. If you can. If you want to..."

He said nothing. Every fiber in his entire body was screaming. He wanted, no *needed*, to break something. Smash something into little pieces like his life had been when she'd left him all those years ago. To run as fast as he could until he dropped in exhaustion. Wanted to curl up in a ball just like the young boy had when she'd left.

Instead, he turned his back on her and walk across to the far side of the room.

He heard Sophie close the door softly and cross the room to him. Her hand rested lightly on his arm.

"I... I can't talk now." He drew in a deep breath of the cloying air. All the oxygen seemed to have been sucked from the room. He looked around wildly for an escape and saw a back door on the storage room.

"I have to go." He snatched his jacket and guitar and fled through the door, out into the cold night air and the starry night. The moonlight rained down on him, encircling him in a silvery light.

He didn't want light.

He wanted to just disappear.

CHAPTER 19

Beth burst into Sophie's loft early Sunday morning. "Sophie, have you seen this?" She waved her phone in front of Sophie's face.

"What?"

"A video of you and Chase singing Road to Forgiveness. It's gone viral."

"What? Let me see." She snatched the phone from Beth. "Oh my gosh, look at the views." She tapped the play button and watched the video start. "Oh, wow." She stared at the phone as she watched she and Chase sing the song.

"And it keeps jumping up. Look at all those shares." Beth walked over and grabbed a mug and poured herself some coffee.

"I can't believe it."

"Why not? You two were spectacular together. Better than when he sang with that Kimberly person."

"No, we weren't."

"I know you're my best friend, but I'm telling you the truth. It was magical."

Sophie felt a wide grin spread across her face. "I had such a great time. I'd forgotten how much I love to perform. I miss it."

"Music is you, Sophie. You should find a way to get it back in your life."

"I don't have time with the gallery and everything."

"I'm telling you, you're meant to sing." Beth took a sip of coffee. "Oh, hey. Did you find out why Chase froze on stage? He did freeze again, didn't he? Before you came out and joined him?"

Sophie sighed. "He did freeze and I did find out what the problem was—or maybe still is. You know how we were just talking about how well I thought I knew him?"

"Yes, you said you'd gotten to know the real Chase."

"Well, let's just say I was mistaken. I don't really know him at all."

"The freezing thing? You going to get to that?" Beth looked at her from over her mug.

"Right. That. Well, he saw his mother in the audience."

"So?"

"So… he hasn't seen her in over twenty-something years. She left him and his father. Right after his brother died."

"Oh, wow. I've never heard about any of this. Wasn't in anything I read when I searched on the net."

"I'm pretty sure no one really knows. He obviously doesn't tell anyone. He implied to me that she was dead."

"But she just showed up in Sweet River Falls?"

"I guess she showed up in Albuquerque, too."

"The first concert he cancelled? The one where he walked off stage?"

"The very one."

"Hm… I guess everyone has their secrets." Beth shrugged.

"Well, it sure goes to show that I don't know him. I thought his mother was dead and didn't even know he'd ever had a brother." Sophie walked to the window. "And that's not all. His

173

mother showed up at the dressing room after the show."

"Really? How did that go?"

"It didn't. He wouldn't talk to her. I mean, I can't blame him. She left him and just disappeared. But you should have seen the look in her eyes. She was drinking him in. Studying every inch of him like she was taking a mental photo of him to keep with her forever." She took a sip of her coffee and looked out over the river below her. "His mom said she was sorry. Though really, sorry doesn't work for something like that, does it?"

"No, it doesn't. I can't imagine a mother abandoning her child." Beth walked over to stand beside her.

"Then... after his mother left, he just shut down and wouldn't talk to me. He just disappeared into the night." She sighed. "I wanted to talk to him, help him. But he just shut me out."

She turned to look at Beth. "And that was after he *kissed* me Friday night. I thought we were getting closer."

"You are."

"But don't you see? I thought I knew him. I thought maybe... Well, I don't know what I thought. Anyway, I know better than to open up so quickly to someone like I did with Chase. It was foolish. It takes time to get to know someone. I've only known him a few weeks. But, well, I don't really know him, do I? I just thought... well, I thought we connected on some level."

"What you mean is you're falling for him."

"I am not." She almost stomped her foot.

"You already have." Beth draped an arm around her shoulder.

"I can't..." she whispered. "He's leaving."

She stared out at the rushing river below. "Or maybe he's already gone."

CHASE GRABBED the last of his clothes from the dresser and slammed the drawer. He threw the clothes next to his suitcase on the bed. He was done with Sweet River Falls. He couldn't stay here any longer and chance running into his mother—*that woman*—again.

Though, if he left, he wouldn't see Sophie again. He grabbed a handful of clothes and crammed them into the suitcase.

The crushing weight of wanting to leave

and wanting to stay smashed all the breath out of him. He sank onto the bed and stared at the well-worn pine plank floor. As if that was going to provide him with any answers. He scowled at the floor.

His cell phone rang and he dug around in the clothes strewn on the bed until he found it. He looked at the screen. Sam. He was tempted to just not answer, but he knew Sam would just keep calling. He finally tapped the button. "Yes?"

"Chase, have you seen all the media coverage?"

"What are you talking about?"

"Who was that girl?"

"What girl?"

"The one you sang with last night."

Chase scowled. "How do you know about that?"

"It's all over the internet. Social media. The news stations. A video of you guys singing Road to Forgiveness. You guys rocked it."

"I don't get it. It wasn't that large of a crowd. Just a small arena in an out-of-the-way town."

"Chase, listen to me. It's a new world, buddy. Someone took a video of you two singing. Posted it online. It was shared and liked and whatever else people do to things like this. You two are everywhere. My phone hasn't stopped ringing."

He frowned. He didn't need Sam saying people were calling him. He needed to get away for a while.

Alone.

Far, far from Colorado.

"So, can you talk to the woman?"

"What woman?" His mind was still on his mother.

"The girl."

"Sophie."

"Yes, Sophie. Talk to her." Sam's voice came through half demanding and half pleading.

"Talk to her about what?"

"Singing with you again."

"Oh, she's not really a performer. She runs an art gallery."

"She's a singer all right. And a darn good one. Think she'd sing with you again?"

"She has a life here. One that doesn't involve singing."

"But could you talk to her? Ask if she wants to sing with you again?"

"No. I can't." He was too busy trying to get out of this town.

"I have the chairman of the Kids Cancer Group calling and asking if you and this mystery woman would do a benefit concert in Denver next week. Jackson Dillion was scheduled to do it, but he's still in the hospital. They provide trips to the mountains for kids with cancer and their families. A chance for a brief getaway from the chaos and medical procedures and pain they're going through. I know that's one of your favorite charities."

Sam was one of the few people who knew he contributed to that charity, and it was giving Sam an unfair advantage. Chase didn't know how he could turn them down.

He laid back on the bed and stared at the ceiling. He knew the group well. They did a great job. He'd actually donated to them annually after thoroughly checking them out. He would have loved to have a brief time away from the hospitals and doctors and endless stream of medical procedures when Garrett was being treated. A chance to just be a family for a few days without everything centering around the disease.

"So what do you say? You'll talk to her? This Sophie woman?"

He let out a long sigh. "I'll talk to her, but she has her own life. I don't know if she'll want to do this. But I could do it solo if she can't or doesn't want to."

A long pause split the air. "Well... they specifically requested the two of you. A duo. Ride the viral media wave for a bit."

So evidently they didn't want just him solo...

"Ask her and call me back."

Chase dropped the cell phone on the bed. The last thing he needed was something that kept him in Colorado.

GLORIA EDMUNDS PUSHED her way into the Brooks Gallery later that morning. "Sophie, there you are. Did you see the video of you and Chase?"

"I saw it." Sophie put on a welcoming smile even though she didn't really want to *welcome* Gloria...

"I just can't believe it. *You* and Chase Green."

The unmistakable undertone of disbelief and the look that said Sophie didn't deserve the notoriety were clearly echoed in her words.

Gloria was like the tenth person who had popped into the gallery in the last hour to mention the video. Sophie wasn't sure she liked the disruption to her schedule. She had the last day of the show here at the gallery and needed to check on a few things for the wrap up of the Art Weekend. She hadn't planned on singing with Chase or ever imagined a video of them singing would go viral.

Her. Viral. She could barely comprehend the number of people who had heard her sing with Chase.

"I've got to get back to work. Feel free to look around." She turned away from Gloria and noticed that Gloria walked out the door without so much as a look at anything in the gallery.

The door opened again, and Chase came in. A serious look hovered in the corners of his eyes. He did not look happy. "Can we talk?" He walked right up to her.

"Sure, we can go back to my office." She turned to Melissa. "I'll be back in a few minutes. You got this?"

"Got it." Melissa smiled and went to greet some new customers coming into the gallery.

She led Chase back to her office, and he shut the door behind them.

"What did you want to talk about?" She leaned against the corner of her desk.

"You saw the video?"

"I did." She stood back up, wondering what was coming. He was sorry he'd asked her to sing? He was embarrassed by the video?

"Well, I guess it went viral." He scowled.

Not a good sign. "So I've been told. I guess you're upset."

He looked at her then, his eyes widening. "No, I'm not upset. Surprised, but not upset."

"But you're used to singing with professionals."

"Sophie, you were fabulous. You have a beautiful voice."

She blushed in spite of herself, basking in his praise.

"I just need to ask you something."

"What?"

"I… ah… so my manager called." He paced away from her, then turned back. "He wanted to know…"

She waited for him to get to the point.

181

"He wanted to know if you'd sing with me again. At a benefit for the Kids Cancer Group of Denver. There's a concert there this week. Jackson was supposed to sing at it, but, well, he's still in the hospital."

"Me?" She grabbed the back of a chair. "You want me to sing with you again? At a real concert?"

The beginning of a smile played at the corners of his mouth. "Last night was a real concert."

"Well, it was just my hometown, it didn't feel like... oh, I can't even explain myself." She spun the chair around and sank into it.

"Will you do it with me?"

"Why don't you do it alone?"

"Evidently they want both of us. Not me as a solo act."

"I'm sorry. I shouldn't have—"

"You have nothing to apologize for. I froze. You saved me from another embarrassing failure. I literally could not get any words to come into my brain after I saw... that woman."

Pain clearly etched his face, and Sophie's heart squeezed in her chest. She could only imagine what he'd gone through as a young boy when his mother left. How it must still affect him.

Without giving herself time to analyze her decision, she sprang to her feet. "Yes, I'll do the concert with you. It's for a good cause. I can do this." She'd do anything to help erase the pained look on his face.

"Thanks, Sophie. It means a lot to me. The charity means a lot to me. I really appreciate it."

"So, are you going to stay in town until next weekend?" She tried to hide the hope from her voice.

He frowned. "I hadn't thought that far ahead. I was packing when Sam called."

She tried to keep the panic from overwhelming her at the thought of Chase leaving.

"I don't really want to take the chance of running into my mother again."

She walked over and placed her hand on his arm. "I get that. I do. I have no idea of what you went through. But... maybe you should go see her. Talk to her. Get some closure."

"I don't need closure. She finished everything when she left."

"People change, Chase. I can't imagine the pain she must have been going through to lose a child. Maybe leaving was the only way she could deal with it. It doesn't make it right, but a parent should never have to live through the death of their child."

"I don't want to see her again, ever."

"That's your choice to make." She didn't totally understand the pain he must have gone through to lose both his brother and his mother, but she did know one thing. If she had the chance to talk to her own mother one more time, nothing in the world could stop her.

"That's right. My choice. Not my mother's choice."

"Think about it, though. It might help you find some peace about the whole situation."

"I will never make peace with the fact my mother deserted me." He turned and walked out of her office.

She walked over and sank into her desk chair. She had no clue if he was leaving town or sticking around.

Too late, she realized they hadn't even talked about rehearsals for the concert, and she really didn't want to fly blindly into it like she had at the concert in Sweet River Falls.

CHAPTER 20

Beth walked arm in arm with Sophie as they headed to Antonio's for dinner that evening. The boys skipped ahead of them, happy to be going to dinner with their mother. She'd promised them that nothing would stop this dinner out tonight, and she meant it.

Beth turned to Sophie. "So you don't know if Chase stayed in town or not?"

"No, he just left this afternoon without telling me."

"I still think it's fabulous that you're going to do that benefit concert with him this coming weekend."

"Well, I'd love to practice with his band. Surely he'll call me and set that up, right? I don't want to just wing it in front of all those people."

"You did a fabulous job winging it last night."

"That was different. It was just singing for Sweet River Falls."

"Whatever you say." Beth glanced at the boys. "Hey, boys, slow down."

"Hurry up, Mom." Trevor skipped back towards them. "I'm starving."

Connor stopped until they caught up with him. "He's not really starving. Not for real starving."

"Am too."

"Are not."

"Boys." She used her best mom-warning voice.

Just then, Mr. Dobbs rounded the corner and hurried up to them. "There you are."

"There I am." She eyed Dobbs, wondering what he wanted this time.

"We called an emergency meeting of the town council."

"When is it?"

"It's tonight. Starting in twenty minutes. We tried to text you."

She grabbed her phone, and sure enough, she had three missed texts.

The boys looked at her. She could see the disappointment clouding their eyes. She turned to Dobbs. "I'm afraid I can't make it."

"Why not?"

"I'm taking my sons to Antonio's for dinner."

"You go ahead and do what you have to do. I'll take the boys to Antonio's for you," Sophie offered.

"Thanks, Soph, but I promised we'd have a night out. We're going to. It's been forever since the boys and I went to Antonio's."

"And Miss Sophie loves Antonio's, too," Trevor piped up.

"The meeting is important." Dobbs eyed her.

"I'm sure it is, but so is keeping my promise to the boys. I'm afraid I'll have to miss this one. I'll get the minutes of the meeting tomorrow."

"This isn't going to look good for you." Dobbs cocked his head and looked at her with a disapproving look on his face.

"Maybe not, but that's my decision. The council will just have to meet without me."

A self-satisfied smirk crossed his face. "Well,

I'll be sure to tell them that you were unwilling to change your… *dinner plans*."

"You do that."

Connor looked at her. "Does this mean that we're really going to go to Antonio's? You're not just gonna send us with Miss Sophie?"

"That's what it means."

Trevor did a fist pump and twirled around. "Yes!"

She linked her arm with Sophie's again. "Evening, Mr. Dobbs."

With that, they headed down the sidewalk, the boys scampering ahead and back, clearly thrilled that she hadn't deserted them once again.

And so was she.

BETH GATHERED up the shamble of items that seemed to follow in the boys' wake. They'd had a fabulous time at Antonio's, and she'd actually gotten them in bed on time tonight. She placed their shoes by the front door so they'd be easy to find in the morning. Well, she put three shoes there. She still hadn't located one of Trevor's.

A short knock at the door surprised her, and

she glanced at her watch. It was getting late. She opened the door to see Mac standing there, a lopsided grin on his face.

"I know it's late, but I missed you." He stepped inside and swept her up in a hug. "I've hardly seen you in days."

She looked up at him and smiled. "So you drove all the way over here to hug me?"

"Heck, no, woman. I came for a kiss." He grinned and leaned down. His lips brushed hers. He pulled away slightly, still keeping her in his arms. "So, you got a half hour or so for your best guy?"

"I do." She led him over to the couch.

"Did you get your dinner with the boys?" Mac leaned against the back of the couch and draped an arm around her, pulling her close to his side.

"I did. Though we ran into Dobbs who wanted me to come to an emergency town council meeting."

"And?" Mac cocked his head.

"And I said I had plans with the boys."

"You missed the meeting?"

She could hear the surprise in his voice. "I did. And I've been thinking…"

"Thinking what?"

"That maybe… I mean I'm not *sure* yet. But, maybe I should pull out of the mayoral race."

Mac didn't say a word but cocked his head to stare at her.

"I'd feel guilty if I do withdraw. I mean, what might happen to Lone Elk Lake if James Weaver gets elected? He'll do whatever Dobbs wants him to, and he'll have a seat on the zoning committee."

"It's not your lone responsibility to save the lake."

"But Mom is depending on me."

Mac looked directly at her. "No, she isn't, really. She'll find a way to block the rezoning or she'll deal with it if it does pass. She'd always want you to do what's best for you."

"I do feel like I haven't had enough time for the boys, and it would probably only get worse if I get elected."

"Probably."

"And they have to be my first priority."

"Adulting is hard, isn't it?" He gave her a little smile and squeezed her hand.

"What do you think I should do?" She looked at him.

"I think only you can make that decision,

but you know I'm one hundred percent behind anything you decide."

She reached out and touched his face, the slight roughness of a day's whiskers coarse beneath her fingertips. "I can always count on you, can't I?"

"Always." He pulled her close to his side again, and they sat in silence while thoughts whirled through her mind as she tried to make her decision.

CHAPTER 21

The next evening Melissa poked her head into Sophie's office. "You okay? You've been awfully quiet today."

"I'm fine." Sophie sighed. "Just trying to get caught up on gallery business. I spent so much time on the Art Weekend that I got behind on gallery stuff."

"Why don't you let me do some of it for you?" Melissa walked over to the desk. "There, I can log in the new items. And I'll total up the weekend sales for you, too."

Sophie looked gratefully at Melissa. "Really?"

"Of course. I used to do those things for your mother all the time. I know you've been trying to learn everything and do everything, but I really could help you more."

Sophie looked at Melissa. The woman was right. Melissa knew so much about running the gallery. She should let her help out more. Before she could change her mind and insist she could do everything herself, she stood. "I accept your help. I'm exhausted. I think I'll go on upstairs to the loft. Call me if you need me for anything."

"I will. Now go relax." Melissa shooed her out the door.

Sophie wandered upstairs and stood looking out over the river, consciously remembering that the last time she stood here Chase had kissed her. She hadn't heard a word from him since he'd asked her to sing with him in Denver. No details. Nothing about practice sessions.

Maybe he'd changed his mind.

Maybe he wasn't even in town anymore.

She took a sip of her wine and turned to go make something for dinner. She stared into the refrigerator thinking there wasn't a single thing to make in there that appealed to her. With a sigh, she grabbed a wedge of cheese and an apple. Cheese and crackers and apple slices. That was meal enough.

She carefully arranged the items on the

plate. She couldn't help herself. She needed it to look... artful. Picking up the plate, she headed for the chairs in front of the window.

A knock at the door echoed through the apartment. She set the plate back on the counter and crossed over to open the door.

"Hi." Chase stood in the open doorway.

"I didn't know if you were even still in town." She couldn't keep the reproach from entering her voice.

"I know. I'm sorry. I've just been..." He paused. "Can I come in?"

She wasn't sure whether she wanted him to come in or not. He'd basically walked away from her. Twice. After kissing her. Just thinking about him balled her thoughts up in a wad of crumpled emotions.

She realized he was still standing there, waiting patiently for her answer.

"Sure." Was she sure? "Come in."

She stood aside and he entered, brushing dangerously close to her as he stepped past. She closed the door behind him and walked over to the kitchen area. "I was just going to eat. It's not much. Just cheese and apples. Want some?"

"No, I'm fine." He walked over to lean

against the counter. "I expect you're pretty mad at me right now."

"I'm not mad." Well, she was a little bit. "I'm more confused."

"You have every right to be. I've treated you terribly. I'm sorry. I'm just… so confused myself. Seeing my mother…"

"It must have been hard to see her after all this time."

"It was. It is. I mean…" He raked his hand through his hair. "I don't want anything to do with her. Nothing."

He pushed off the counter and walked over to look out the window. "And yet, she's my mother. I kind of feel like the little boy who has waited forever for his mother to return. And now she has. It's like on Christmas morning, seeing that you got exactly what you wanted. Only…"

She walked over to stand beside him. "I'm sure it's confusing."

"But what does she want from me? She left me."

"You could go talk to her. Find out what she wants."

"But I'm so angry at her. I don't know if I can even talk to her without…" He turned to look at Sophie. "I might lose my temper and say something that can't be taken back."

Sophie reached out and took his hand in hers. "I can't decide this for you. All I know is that if I had a chance to see my mother again... We don't always get second chances in life. You have that chance. Maybe you can see her and find some kind of peace."

"Maybe."

"So you'll go see her?"

"I think so. Maybe I can find some peace with all of this even if we just talk this one time."

"I hope you can. Why don't you go now? Before you have time to change your mind."

He gave her a weak smile. "You're a pushy one, aren't you?"

"I just think she's come to see you twice now. She wants to connect. You could at least listen to what she has to say."

"Okay. I will. I'll go over to the Pine View B&B and see if she's still there."

"I bet she is." Sophie led him back to the door.

He stood by the open door and took both her hands in his. "Thank you. For listening. For being patient with me. For forgiving me for how

I've treated you the last few days. I didn't mean to hurt you."

He reached out and she felt the warmth of his hand on her face. She pressed her hand against his.

"Sophie?"

"Yes?"

"I… care about you. I didn't mean to hurt you. We should talk soon and sort things out."

"I'd like that. But right now, go see your mother. See if you can sort that out first."

She thought he might kiss her then, but he slowly pulled his hand back and gave her the look of a little lost boy. He turned and slowly trudged down the stairs and out into the growing darkness of the Colorado evening.

CHASE STOOD at the front door of the Pine View Bed and Breakfast. Warm light spilled out onto the wide front porch. He could see a cheery fire through the front window. He moved to get a better look, feeling a bit like a stalker. He froze in place.

His mother sat in a chair near the fire. She was knitting something. She knits now. He tucked that fact in his brain. He'd never seen her knit in all the time she'd been… well, when she'd been with him and her family.

Just then the door opened and a petite blonde woman stood in the doorway. "Well, hello there. May I help you?"

"Um, yes. I came to see Elizabeth Green."

"Liz?"

Well, that was new, too. His mother had always gone by the full name Elizabeth. No nickname.

He just nodded at the woman.

The woman gave him a warm smile. "I'm Lucy Compton."

"Nice to meet you, Lucy."

"Why don't you come in? Liz is sitting by the fire. We were just chatting a bit."

Lucy turned and headed inside. He stood frozen on the porch. She poked her head back out. "You coming?"

"I'm coming." He forced himself to take a step. And another one. And one more. Soon he was inside the cheerful building.

Lucy led him to the front room. "Liz is in there. I'll leave you two alone."

His mother rose as soon as she saw him, her knitting falling to the floor. "Chase."

He stepped into the room. "I hear you go by Liz now."

She bent down and scooped up her knitting and set it on a table by her chair. "I do. I needed a change."

"Lots of change. Like leaving your family behind change."

"Chase, I'm so sorry for that. For leaving you."

"Sorry? You think saying you're sorry makes any difference at all?"

"I don't suppose it does. But I do want you to know that I am sorry. It's the biggest regret of my life."

"Why did you leave?" He couldn't believe he was finally getting the chance to ask her that question, in person, to her face.

"I felt like I had to. When Garrett..." She pushed her hair away from her face. "When he died, I felt so empty, so lost. I felt like the whole world was crushing me and I couldn't take a breath."

"So did I. I lost my brother, my best friend."

"I know you did. I should have been there for you to help you through it. At the time all I could think of was to run away. As if running away would get me further from the pain." She took a step toward him. "Your father blamed me, you know."

"No, he didn't." Chase frowned.

"He did. He thought I should have realized something was wrong with Garrett sooner. He told me that I should have taken him to the doctor when he first got sick. I didn't, you know. I thought it was nothing. Just some kind of kid's bug he'd picked up that was lingering on longer than normal."

Chase frowned. He didn't remember any of this, though he knew his father had been angry when Garrett was ill. But he figured it was just a reaction to the helplessness they all felt. He tried to think back on that time, something he rarely let himself do. He remembered his mother started sleeping in the guest room, but he'd thought that it was because it was right next to Garrett's room, so she could hear him if he needed her.

"I'll never forgive myself for not taking him in to see the doctor sooner."

"You don't know that it would have made a difference."

A lone tear trailed down his mother's cheek. "No, I won't ever know for sure. But I didn't give him that chance. That chance that things might have been caught earlier. What kind of mother just puts off taking her child in when he's sick? I wasn't a doctor. I shouldn't have made that choice of thinking it was nothing."

"So you've blamed yourself all these years?"

"I do blame myself." She swiped away the tear. "And what if I made another bad decision that affected your life? I wasn't fit to be a mother…"

A memory long hidden came flooding back to him. The night before Garrett's funeral. His parents arguing downstairs. His father's words had thundered through the house. That's exactly what his dad had said to his mother. *She wasn't fit to be a mother.*

"I know that none of this excuses me leaving you. I was in so much pain and had so much guilt. So I ran away… It wasn't right, but it was the choice I made at the time, and I can't change it now. I'm so very sorry for leaving you, though. I am."

His thoughts and his words tangled in his brain and he stood there staring at her as she crossed the distance between them. She reached out to touch him, and a war broke out inside of him. The little boy who wanted to throw himself into his mother's arms and be comforted and the man who had lived years without his mother, not knowing why she left him.

"Chase?" She looked at him questioningly.

He still couldn't find a single word to say.

She opened her arms to him, but still, he stood.

"I don't expect you to forgive me. What I did was unforgivable. But… if I could just hold you one more time…"

The man side of him began to realize what had motivated her to leave all those years ago. Could understand the guilt and grief she'd been carrying with her. He didn't exactly forgive her, but at least there was a hint of understanding.

The war ended, and he walked into his mother's embrace.

CHAPTER 22

Beth sat at the kitchen table at her mother's cabin, watching her mother finish cleaning up after one of her famous baking extravaganzas. Her mother was always baking or cooking something, along with running the lodge. She never could figure out how her mother juggled everything so smoothly.

She didn't juggle things smoothly. Not in the least. A trait she hadn't inherited from her mother, though she wished she had.

She sipped her coffee, trying to get up her nerve to tell her mother why she'd come over.

Her mother looked at her and laughed. "You might as well just come out and say it."

"Say what?" She eyed her mother.

"Say whatever it is that you've been trying to tell me for the last five minutes."

"How do you…" Beth shook her head. "Never mind. You always know when I need to talk."

"So what is it?"

She took a deep breath. "Mom, I know I'm letting you down, but I need to withdraw from the race for mayor."

"Good." Her mother set down a hot loaf of homemade bread on a cooling rack.

"Good?"

"Yes, good. I'd never stand in your way of anything you wanted to do, you know that. I know you can do anything that you set your mind to. But sometimes… well, you take on a lot. You don't always know how to say no."

Beth sighed. "You're right. It's just when I heard James Weaver saying he was running unopposed and I knew that meant it was going to be harder to stop any zoning changes to the lake… Well, I had to do something."

"And we will. We'll try everything we can to keep the lake the way it is. But it doesn't mean you have to give up your time with the boys. Being a Mom is hard. It means tough choices.

And you'll never regret giving up something so you have more time with them. Kids grow up so quickly."

"They do. I still can't believe they aren't little toddlers. Connor seems so old sometimes."

"But he's still a young boy who needs his mother."

"I know. And I'm busy enough with my teaching job, then helping out here at the lodge during the busy summer season. And I feel like I'm always asking you for help with the boys."

"You know I never mind helping you out with them. I love spending time with the boys."

"And they love spending time with you. But, honestly? I miss them. I've just been so busy with campaigning and making sure I go to this meeting and that meeting."

"So, when are you going to officially withdraw?"

"I guess I'll head into town now. I really hate to disappoint you, Mom."

"You're not disappointing me." Her mom sat down beside her and put her hand over Beth's. "I'm always so proud of you. All that you've accomplished. What a wonderful mother you are."

"Thanks, Mom." Beth didn't know what she'd done to get such a terrific mother, but she was grateful every single day for having her mom in her life. She knew that Sophie missed her mom terribly.

"Finish up that coffee and go on your way. You'll feel better after you actually withdraw." Her mom stood back up. "And don't worry about me. We'll find a way to fight any changes to the lake."

"I hope so." She got up and set her cup in the sink. "Okay, I'm doing this now. Before I change my mind." Not that she was going to change her decision. She was sure she was making the right choice.

Pretty sure.

BETH PUSHED OPEN the door to city hall. She just needed to turn in the letter she'd written stating she was withdrawing from the mayoral race. Hopefully, she could just quickly give it to the secretary and escape back outside without running into anyone. Soon enough everyone would know she was out of the race.

She walked to the desk and smiled at the

woman working there. "I just need to turn in this letter."

The woman glanced at the envelope. "To the election committee?"

"Yes."

"Okay, I'll make sure they get it."

"Thank you." Beth turned around, and much to her dismay, Dobbs was just entering the building.

"Well, well, Miss Cassidy. What brings you to city hall?"

"I—" She took a deep breath and looked right at him. "I'm turning in my official letter that I'm withdrawing from the mayoral race."

She couldn't miss the wide grin that spread across Dobbs's face. "Are you, now?" The grin got wider if that was even possible.

"Yes. I'm afraid so."

"Well, it looks like James Weaver will be our next mayor then. Of course, I was sure he would be anyway, even if you were in the race."

Of course, Dobbs thought that. But it didn't matter now because James would be running unopposed.

"Of course, we'll still have the election. Have to give the town the opportunity to show their support for James. And there's the option for write-in candidates." Dobbs rubbed his hands together in glee. "I best go find James and tell him the good news."

Dobbs spun around and headed out the door.

Beth stood in the entryway for a moment, unsure of how she felt about everything. Then she straightened her shoulders and pushed back outside. The decision was made. James Weaver would be the next mayor.

She decided to tell Sophie the news and hurried down the street to the gallery. She waved to Melissa as she entered. Melissa pointed to the back room, and Beth headed that direction.

"Hey, Soph."

Sophie turned at the sound of her voice. "Hey, Beth. What's up?"

"How do you know something is up?"

"You have that I-need-to-talk look on your face."

"Man, you and my mother. I can't hide anything from you two."

"So, what gives?" Sophie put down a stack of papers and gave Beth her full attention.

"So... I just turned in my letter withdrawing from the mayoral race."

"Good."

Beth laughed. "That's exactly what my mother said."

"Of course she did. You're trying to be all things to everyone, but you're just one person. You always sign on to do too much."

"Gee, thanks for your support."

Sophie laughed and hugged her. "You know what I mean. I'd support you in anything you wanted to do, but in this instance, I'm glad you decided to back off."

"I'm still worried about Mom and the lake."

"I'm sure Nora will do everything she can to stop Dobbs from pushing through his zoning change."

"But James will be on the zoning committee since he'll be the mayor, and he does everything Dobbs tells him to. He's basically a puppet for Dobbs."

"Well, we'll just have to raise more support to stop them. I'll do everything I can to help."

"Thanks." Beth sank onto a chair. "I just feel like I'm letting Mom down. Letting down everyone who enjoys Lone Elk Lake just like it is."

"How long are you going to beat yourself up

for making this decision?" Sophie cocked her head to one side and eyed Beth.

Beth laughed again. "You're right. The decision is made, and I know it was the right one for the boys and for me."

"And that's the important thing." Sophie dipped her head in emphasis.

"So speaking of decisions. What's up with you and Chase?"

Sophie sat in the chair across from her. "Well, he came by last night."

"And?"

"And I convinced him to go see his mother."

"Really?" Beth eyed her friend.

"I did. I think he needed to talk to her to find some kind of peace with the whole situation. Maybe hear her side. Or maybe just yell at her for leaving him." Sophie shrugged.

"Well, I hope it helps."

"Then he said we should talk."

"You and him? What about?"

"The concert… us… I'm just not sure."

"High time. You two need to sort it out. You need to tell him how you feel about him."

"But I'm not sure I know how I feel about him."

Beth shook her head. "Sure you do. You're

just not ready to admit it to yourself yet." Beth glanced at her watch and stood up. "Well, I better go pick the boys up from after-school sports and let them know they no longer have a chance of being the sons of the mayor of Sweet River Falls."

"I bet they'll be thrilled."

"I might even celebrate with them by making homemade pizza."

"Good choice."

"I'm making lots of good choices these days." A grin spread across her face. "You should make a good choice about Chase."

SOPHIE WALKED Beth to the door of the gallery. Beth opened the door and Chase stood in the doorway. "Well, hello there. Coming to see Soph?"

"I am." His deep voice wrapped around Sophie. She was so glad to see him again and couldn't wait to hear what happened with his mother.

Beth gave Sophie an expectant look. She knew exactly what Beth was saying with that look. *Talk to the man.*

"I'm outta here." Beth slipped through the door leaving Sophie and Chase standing looking at each other.

"Come on in. Come back to my office." Sophie tugged Chase's hand and led him to the back of the gallery. She perched on a chair and waited for him to talk, though she was dying to ask him about his mother.

"So, if it works with your schedule, we could head to Denver the end of the week. Have a day of practice before the concert?"

"That works for me. I already talked to Melissa about running the gallery while I'm gone. We're calling in some other part-time workers to help her out."

"Good. Glad that works for you. We'll do the same numbers we did here in Sweet River Falls, plus I'd like to add a few more. Here, I brought you the music." He handed her a folder.

She leafed through the folder and recognized most of the songs. She just needed to make sure she knew all the words.

"Here's a flash drive with the songs on it." He handed it to her.

"I'll listen to them tonight. I think I know most of these."

"If we had more time, we could learn some new songs I've written. But, well, time isn't something we have. The last two songs on the drive are new ones. Don't worry if you don't learn those. We'll go with the old standbys."

She nodded. It was all starting to get real. She was going to do a concert with Chase Green. A real one. Not just happening into one like last weekend.

"You sure you're okay with all of this?" He looked at her.

"I'm sure. I mean I think I'm sure." She grinned at him.

"And one other thing." Chase reached out his hands and pulled her to her feet. "I've been wanting to kiss you again for what seems like forever."

"I think it's been a very, very long time." She tried to keep a serious expression.

"Ah, well, we should remedy that."

"We probably should." She nodded, deciding to just deal with whatever ended up happening later. Because kissing Chase was just so very nice…

He grinned, then leaned close and kissed her gently. She circled her arms around his neck.

When he finally stopped kissing her, she stood in front of him, slightly dazed.

"We should do that more often." He flashed a lazy grin at her.

Yes, they definitely should...

CHAPTER 23

C hase stood by her side backstage, waiting for the concert to begin. Her nerves were frazzled, and she kept running through the words to the songs they were going to sing.

He looked down at her. "You nervous?"

"A bit. Okay, a lot. This is all so new to me."

"You'll do great. You rocked the practices yesterday."

"What if I forget the words?"

"Fake it." He grinned.

"You might as well be doing this solo then."

A flash of something crossed his face, but she was too nervous to figure out what the look meant.

The announcer came on and introduced

them. The band started up. It was time. She pressed her palms against her legs.

"Okay, you ready?" He looked encouragingly at her.

She nodded, unable to speak. Which wasn't a good sign since they were supposed to go out there into those bright lights and start singing.

He took her hand in his and led her out onto the stage. The lights flooded around them. The crowd soared to their feet and started clapping. The noise level rose to an unbelievable level.

Chase waved to the crowd.

She didn't.

She smiled weakly.

The band started the intro to their first song. She heard Chase sing the first verse and got ready to join him on the chorus, just like they'd rehearsed. He started into the chorus, and to her surprise, she heard her voice joining in with him.

She could do this.

She could.

She didn't know how long they stayed out there on stage singing, including two encores. The night blurred past her, taking her on a high she'd never experienced before. Singing for all these people. Listening to the applause.

And seeing Chase smile at her through it all. Hearing him sing in his low, throaty voice. She could almost imagine he was singing those flirty love songs to her. Really to her. But that was silly. It was all showmanship.

He finally took her hand and they walked off the stage. Once they got out of the lights, he swooped her up in the tight hug, her feet lifting off the ground as he spun in a circle. "You were fabulous, Sophie." His eyes shone with the excitement of the night.

She wasn't sure she ever wanted him to let her down.

Chase set her back on the ground when the charity event chairman walked up to them. The man held out his hand. "I can't thank you two enough. A sold-out crowd. And more donations to the charity are being made as the crowd leaves the arena. You've done a really great thing to help so many families going through a rough time with childhood cancer."

"We were happy to help." Chase shook the man's hand.

"Yes, we were glad we could do this." She smiled at the man.

"You're coming to the after party? We have a lot of the big donors coming there. They'd love to meet you."

"You up for it, Sophie?" Chase looked at her.

"I think so." She was floating so high she didn't know if she could have a coherent conversation with anyone, but if Chase wanted to go, she wanted to go with him.

"I'll have a car pick you up in, say, thirty minutes?" The man looked at them.

"Thirty minutes it is." Chase took her hand and led her back toward the dressing rooms.

Real dressing rooms. Not just some storage room off the edge of the stage like when they'd sung in Sweet River Falls. This one even had her name on the door. Okay, it was only on a printed piece of paper, but it was *her name on the door*.

CHASE MADE his way through the crowd with two glasses of champagne in his hands. He'd last seen Sophie talking to a couple of the guys from the band and promised he'd bring her a drink. That had been at least thirty minutes and a dozen interruptions of people stopping him to talk while he wound his way back to her.

She was nowhere to be found when he got back to where he'd last seen her. He scanned the crowd.

Then he saw her. Saw them. Sophie was standing in the far corner talking to his mother. He resolutely threaded his way through the crowd, headed in their direction, once again getting stopped every step of the way. He was careful to be gracious, but he wanted to get to Sophie.

He finally was just a few steps from her. "Sophie."

She turned and smiled at him.

Just then Sam rushed up to them. "Chase. Sophie. That was great. Just great. Check out the social media coverage you're already getting." He waved his cell phone in front of them. "You two are going to be the next big thing. Trust me. I know this."

"Hi, Sam." Chase looked at his friend and shook his head. "I think you're exaggerating."

"Nope, I'm not." Sam looked at Chase's mom with a questioning look.

"Sam, you met Sophie yesterday, but this is my mother, Elizabeth—Liz—Green."

He didn't miss the surprised look in Sam's eyes. "Ah, Mrs. Green, so nice to meet you."

"Nice to meet you." His mother smiled. "They were wonderful, weren't they? I couldn't agree with your assessment any more."

"Yep, next big thing." Sam waved at someone in the distance. "Gotta go do some promo for you." He headed off through the throng of people.

"I appreciate you getting me such a great ticket, Chase." His mom smiled at him.

He'd been just fine with her sitting in the front row this time. Hadn't frozen. It had almost seemed perfectly normal to have her there listening to them. Almost. "Hope you enjoyed it."

"Very much." She turned to Sophie. "And I've enjoyed chatting with Sophie. You two really are great together. Singing, I mean."

"Thank you." Sophie blushed.

Of course she did. She was always turning rosy when people complimented her. He looked at her and realized she looked exhausted. He recognized that look. The crash of coming down after the high of a performance.

"How about we get out of here and head back to the hotel?"

Sophie nodded gratefully. "I am getting tired."

"I'm heading out now, too. Thank you for inviting me to come." His mother turned and walked away before he could even ask where she was staying or if she was headed back to Sweet River Falls. For that matter, he didn't have her address or phone number.

He whirled around and searched the crowd, but it had swallowed her, and he saw no sign of her.

"You okay?" Sophie frowned.

"Yes… I just. It's nothing." He just wasn't sure he'd ever see his mother again. She hadn't said a word about seeing him again. Maybe she'd just disappear like the last time.

"Let's go." He grabbed Sophie's hand and led her through the crowd.

CHAPTER 24

Sophie and Chase headed back to Sweet River Falls early the next morning. Sophie barely said a word on the drive. He wasn't sure if it was because she was still exhausted or whether it was the three calls from Sam, telling them how many media outlets had picked up a story about them singing together. Maybe she was overwhelmed. He didn't blame her. He was a bit overwhelmed himself.

This isn't what he'd planned. He was going out solo. His success would not depend on anyone else or their choices or decisions.

And yet, here they were, an almost overnight success.

Sam had said his phone was ringing

constantly with offers to book them. As a duo. Not him as a solo.

He looked over at her as she stared out her window. He wanted to reach over and tuck a wayward lock of hair behind her ear but didn't want to disturb her. He smiled to himself. He'd had a wonderful time singing with her. So different than when he performed with Kimberly. Sophie had obviously enjoyed herself, enjoyed *the music*. He'd always thought that Kimberly was more about the performance than the music. She always wanted to sparkle for the audience.

But Sophie was more like him. The music spoke to her like it did to him. He could tell that in the way she sang.

He pulled down Main Street and parked by the gallery. She finally turned to look at him.

"You okay? You were awfully quiet."

"It was a long night. It was wonderful and different and overwhelming."

"Come on, I'll grab your bag and walk you upstairs."

"I can get it. I need to check in with Melissa first anyway. See how things went at the gallery while I was gone."

He climbed out of the car and grabbed her

bag. She came around and took it from him. They stood in awkward silence.

"I... Could I come over tonight? We should talk." Chase reached out to set his hand on her hand resting on the handle of the suitcase.

"I'm tired, Chase. Really tired."

His heart slipped in his chest. Things were getting messed up between them. He could feel it.

"Okay. Well, maybe tomorrow, then."

She looked at him and sighed. "No, later this evening would be fine. Just let me deal with work first."

She turned and disappeared into the gallery. He stood on the sidewalk for a long time, just staring at the window of the gallery, not really seeing anything.

SOPHIE OPENED the door at Chase's knock. He looked refreshed and... did he look nervous?

"Come in."

He slipped inside.

"I thought we—"

"We should—"

They both started talking at the same time.

Chase paused and gave her a rueful smile. "You first."

"No, you go ahead." Because she didn't really know what she was going to say to him.

"So, as you know, Sam says he's been flooded with offers. People wanting us to perform. Together. And not just for charity events. We've gotten some pretty good offers."

"But… I'm not a real singer." Only she'd *felt* like a real singer even if she had a hard time admitting that to herself.

"What do you think a *real* singer is? You went on stage. You sang. People loved you. You loved the music, I know you did."

"I did… but, well, I'm a gallery owner."

"So you didn't enjoy singing with me?"

"Of course I did. It was wonderful." It was more than wonderful. It had filled some special place inside of her that she'd thought would never be filled again.

"Wouldn't you like to do it some more? Sam has offered to be your manager, too. Or we could find you someone else if you'd rather."

"I just can't abandon the gallery. I can't. I won't let my parents down."

"How is it letting them down if you decide

to go after your dreams?" He reached out to touch her.

She avoided his touch and crossed over to the window. Unable to look at him and tell him the truth.

She felt him come up and stand behind her. His arms circled around her waist. "Talk to me, Sophie."

She didn't want to talk to him. To explain. And yet she did want to. Her thoughts tangled. "It's my... fault..." She tripped over her words. "It's my fault they're gone. So don't you see? I have to keep their dream alive. It's more important than my dreams."

She pulled out of his arms. "It's my fault they died. They were headed to Denver for the theater. I'd gotten us all tickets to go, but then I'd backed out at the last minute. So they went without me. And... there was a terrible pile-up on the highway, and they were both killed. If I hadn't have gotten the tickets, or if I hadn't backed out... everything would be different." Her hearted pounded in her chest, and guilt and sorrow overwhelmed her.

"I'm sorry, Sophie." His eyes were filled with sympathy.

Sympathy was the last thing she needed it.

She'd brought this all on herself. "The least I can do is keep the gallery going in their name. The very least."

"But, Sophie—"

"No, Chase. It's the right thing to do. I'm sorry. I can't go on the road with you. I can't."

Running the gallery was the only way she knew how to prove to her parents just how sorry she was.

CHAPTER 25

Hunt opened the car door and Keely slipped out. They stood in front of a quaint cabin a short distance from town.

Hunt wrapped Keely in a bear hug. "We did it."

She grinned up at him. "I can't believe we made this decision."

"Here's our home base for the next year." He reached out a hand and led her up to the door. He put the key in the lock, opened the door, and swept her up in his arms.

A laugh escaped her lips. "What are you doing?"

"Carrying you over the threshold."

"That's for the first time you cross the threshold after you're married."

"You're too strict with your rules." He grinned at her, carried her inside, and set her down in the front room.

"This is really nice." She slowly turned around, taking in the whole area.

"It's got an updated kitchen, and a huge porch overlooking an expansive view of the mountains in the distance." He took her hand and they walked through the cabin and out on the porch.

"This is perfect." Though she knew she'd live anywhere with Hunt. "I love Comfort Crossing, but it just feels so... freeing... to finally live somewhere else."

"Well, now we have this cabin all to ourselves. I'm going to do that photo book I've planned, and we'll travel around the Rockies some, but we'll have this cabin to come back to."

"Katherine was thrilled to be put in charge of running Magnolia Cafe." Keely walked over to the railing and stared down into the water. She turned back to him "This *is* perfect. We're going to have the best year."

"Every year with you is perfect." He leaned over and kissed her.

She had to be the luckiest woman in the world.

CHAPTER 26

Beth burst into Sophie's loft the next morning. "You're famous. I know a famous singer." She came over and hugged Sophie then stepped back. "But why do you look like that?"

"Like what?"

"Like you're not as excited about your success as I am." Beth frowned. "Did you have a good time?"

"I loved it. It was so unimaginably wonderful. The music. The people."

"So, what's the problem?"

"Sam—that's Chase's agent—keeps calling Chase telling him about offers that are coming in."

"That's good, right?"

"No, it's not. I mean, this was supposed to be a one-time thing. I have the gallery to run. I can't just head off all over the country anytime I want"

"Sure you can."

"I have responsibilities."

"You can find a way if it's what you really want to do. You know you were born to sing."

Sophie sank into a chair. "I can't leave the gallery. I have to keep it going. Honor my parents' memory."

"You don't think it would honor them if you were a famous singer? Or even a not famous one. You know they would only want you to be happy. That's all they ever wanted."

"But… I can't let them down."

"Sophie, you have this chance. This chance to do what you love."

"But I owe my parents."

"That's nonsense. You don't owe them this. It's time you quit blaming yourself for their accident."

Sophie looked at Beth in surprise. She'd never mentioned the guilt she felt all these years, but somehow Beth knew, which shouldn't surprise her in the least. Sometimes she'd swear that Beth knew her better than she knew herself.

"Sophie, fate is cruel sometimes. Bad things happen to good people. You might have been killed too if you'd gone with them. It was an accident. We can spend our whole lives regretting decisions, but it doesn't change them. Your parents would never blame you for what happened and never want you to feel obligated to run the gallery."

"But—"

Beth shot her a look she usually reserved for scolding Trevor and Connor. "I'm sorry, but weren't you the one who told me that I should do what was right for me when I was trying to decide about pulling out of the race for mayor?"

"That was different."

"How?"

Sophie gave her friend a weak smile. "Because it was advice for *you*?"

"Nice try, Soph."

"Anyway, I know that Chase wanted to go out solo. So me staying here and running the gallery works out the best for everyone."

"Sophie, we get one chance at life. It's our responsibility to make the very best out of every opportunity thrown our way." Beth pinned her a listen-to-me-I'm-the-teacher look. "At least think about it."

~

CHASE SLAMMED AROUND THE CABIN, packing up his things once again. He threw his clothes on the bed in the general direction of his suitcase. He let at least ten calls from Sam go to voicemail. He wasn't ready to talk to him. Maybe he'd never be ready.

Sam wanted Chase and Sophie to sing.

And that was never going to happen. Sophie had made that clear; she'd made her choice.

He also had to come to grips with the fact he was never going to make it as a solo act. And that had been his goal for two years. He never wanted to be dependent on someone else for his success.

Never. Ever.

So he was *fine* with her saying no. Saying she had to stay in Sweet River Falls and run the gallery.

Fine with it. Just fine.

And yet, it seemed like his driving need to be a solo act lessened when he sang with Sophie.

He loved watching her sing.

Loved seeing the joy on her face when they did a duet.

He loved…

He sat down abruptly when the air was suddenly sucked from his lungs and the room spun around him.

He loved…

He loved *her*.

Now the question was, was he going to do anything about it?

CHAPTER 27

C hase's thoughts were interrupted by a knock at the door to his cabin. He climbed off the bed and went to answer it.

"Hello, son."

"Mom." She was the last person he'd expected to see.

"I heard you were staying out here at Sweet River Lodge, and this nice lady at the desk—I think her name was Nora—told me what cabin you were staying in when I told her I was your mother."

"I wasn't sure I'd see you again."

"Well, I hope that we can keep in touch. I'd like to stay part of your life if you'll let me." She looked at him. "Maybe I could come hear you and Sophie sing again."

"That's not going to happen."

"Oh, I'm sorry." A darkness passed over her face and her eyes clouded. "I don't want to intrude on your life. I can't blame you if you don't want to see me." She turned to leave.

He reached out his hand to stop her. "No, Mom, it's not that."

She turned to look at him. "What's wrong, son?"

"I… Sophie doesn't want to sing with me. She feels she needs to stay here and run the gallery. It's a long story but it's all about responsibilities and guilt."

"I'm sorry. I thought you two were brilliant together. I also thought… Well, I thought maybe she had a bit of a crush on you. And honestly, by the way you looked at her, I thought you cared about her, too."

"You some kind of mind reader?" He scowled. "I've just come to that same conclusion myself. I *do* care about her. I care a lot."

"Have you told her that?"

"I don't think it would change things. She has to do what she has to do."

"I think you should go talk to her. Tell her how you feel. You don't want to live to regret a decision you made…"

He wasn't sure if she was talking about his decision or her decision to leave all those years ago.

"Guilt is a hard thing to live with. We all deal with it in different ways. You say she feels guilt? Maybe you can help her deal with it. Maybe she just needs someone to believe in her and help her to forgive herself. It's very hard to learn to forgive."

"You been saving up motherly advice for all these years?"

She gave him a small smile. "All I want is for you to be happy. I think she makes you happy."

"When she isn't driving me crazy."

She smiled again. "Go talk to her."

He reached inside and grabbed his keys off the table by the door. "Okay, I've always heard a person should listen to their mother."

"They should."

He started down the stairs and turned back. "Mom, you going to still be around town for a bit?"

"If you want me to be."

"I do."

"Then I'll stay as long as you need me."

For the first time in a very long time, he felt the love of his mother, her support. And she was right, it was very hard to learn to forgive. Forgive yourself, forgive others. He was going to try his best to find a way to forgive his mother and see if they could build some kind of relationship.

"Wish me luck." He grinned at his mother, and his heart sprang with new hope. Hope about Sophie, hope about a new beginning with his mother.

"Good luck, son."

BETH AND SOPHIE headed downstairs to the gallery. Sophie wasn't sure she was ready to take Beth's advice. She had so many unresolved feelings about her parents' accident. So much guilt. How did a person ever get over that? The guilt over a decision they'd made that had such far-reaching consequences?

"Sophie, there you are." Hunt and Keely came walking up to them.

"Guess what?" Keely was practically beaming.

"What?" Sophie pulled herself away from the thoughts brewing in her head.

"We just leased a cabin up near Grace's Peak for the next year," Hunt announced.

"Here in Sweet River Falls?" Beth looked surprised.

"Yep. Going to make it our home base for a while. I'm going to be working on a photography project with the mountain area. We wanted a bit of a change." Hunt shrugged. "So, we decided to stay."

"And I fell in love with the town." Keely smiled.

"That's fabulous." Sophie reached out to take Keely's hand. "We'll love having you here."

"I was hoping to place more of my work here at the gallery."

"I'd love that."

"Only Sophie may be making changes to the gallery." Beth gave her a isn't-that-right look.

Sophie frowned at her.

"What kind of changes?" Hunt asked.

"Well, she's been offered a chance to sing with Chase Green."

"That's so exciting." Keely squeezed Sophie's hand.

"But I'm not sure…"

Melissa walked up to them. "Seriously, you know that I can hear everything you're saying, right? I think that's wonderful that you have the chance to sing. I know that's what really makes you happy."

"But—"

"I can run the gallery when you're on the road. I know the business side from working with your mother. I don't have her eye for art, but I *do* know the business side."

"I'd be glad to help out too. Have you ever considered taking on a partner? I know this friend of ours who owns a gallery on Belle Island near Lighthouse Point. He's invested in a few galleries around the country. I bet he'd love this one." Hunt swept his gaze around the gallery.

Sophie tried to take in all the talk whirling around her.

"Paul Clark. I could talk to him. He married a lady from Comfort Crossing where we're from."

"But, my parents… it was their dream…"

"You could still keep the name Brooks Gallery. He'd just be able to help with acquiring new art when you're gone. I'll put him in touch with you if you'd like."

"Hey, and I'll be looking for a part-time job

while we're here if you need some more help," Keely added.

Beth looked at her triumphantly. "See, everything works out the way it's supposed to be. Sometimes the universe gives you opportunities that you never expected. I think it's trying to nudge you in the right direction. Now all you have to do is decide to take a chance. Go for it."

Sophie grinned at her very best friend in the whole wide world and hugged her. "You're the best."

"Of course I am. I live to help you make good choices."

Sophie let go of Beth. "I need to find Chase. Tell him I've changed my mind. I want to sing with him."

"While you're there you might want to tell him you love him, too." Beth looked at her pointedly.

A wide grin spread across her face. "Yes, I probably should tell him that, too."

Sophie hurried out the door and ran right into the hard chest of Chase Green. She struggled to catch her breath as he reached out his hands to steady her.

"Sophie, I—"

"Chase, I was—"

"You first this time." He looked down at her and nodded.

She looked straight into his eyes and gathered her courage, sure of her decision. Her heart pounded, and she took a deep breath. "If you still want to... if you want *me*..."

"I do want you, Sophie. More than you know. And not just as my singing partner. If you can't leave here, if you don't want to sing with me, I understand. We'll work it out. But I don't want to lose you."

"But that's what I was coming to tell you."

"Tell me what?" He cocked his head.

"I was coming to say that if you want me to sing with you, then, yes. That's what I want, too. I love singing with you, Chase, I really do. It makes me happy and fulfills me in ways I never thought possible."

"All righty then." He scooped her up and swung her around, her feet flying off the sidewalk in a dizzying spin. "That's the best thing I've heard all day. All year. Maybe in my whole life."

He finally set her back down, and the world still spun crazily around her. She just wasn't sure if it was because of his twirls or the chaos of her emotions.

She reached out and steadied herself on his arm. "But I know you really wanted to try and sing solo…"

He shrugged. "Life throws us curves. Plans change, Sophie. I'd rather have you singing by my side than ever sing solo. You *get* music. How it feels to sing the songs. It moves you like it moves me. It would make me ridiculously happy if you'd sing with me, become my partner."

"Okay, but one more thing, Chase Green." She grinned at him, her heart soaring.

"What's that?" He eyed her with his silly lopsided grin.

"I've fallen in love with you."

His eyes widened and he scooped her up in a twirl again. "Now, *that's* the best thing I've heard in my whole life. For sure."

"Your whole entire life?"

"Yep. And guess what?"

"What?"

"I love you, too, Sophie Brooks. Very much."

He set her down on the sidewalk, then

leaned down and kissed her right there in broad daylight on Main Street in Sweet River Falls.

And suddenly, all was right with her world, and she kissed him right back.

DEAR READER - I hope you enjoyed this story in the Sweet River series. If you want to read about how the characters Hunt and Keely met, check out The Magnolia Cafe in the Comfort Crossing series. (Or start at the beginning of that series with the free series starter The Shop on Main.) Look for more books in the Sweet River series in the coming months.

Sign up for my VIP READERS at my website to be the first to know about new releases, sales, and exclusive promos. Or join my reader group on Facebook. They're always helping me name my characters, see my covers first, and we just generally have a good time.

As always, thanks for reading my stories. I truly appreciate all my readers.

THANK YOU for reading my story. I hope you enjoyed it. Sign up for my newsletter to be updated with information on new releases, promotions, give-aways, and newsletter-only surprises. The signup is at my website, kaycorrell.com.

Reviews help other readers find new books. I always appreciate when my readers take time to leave an honest review.

I love to hear from my readers. Feel free to contact me at authorcontact@kaycorrell.com

COMFORT CROSSING ~ THE SERIES

The Shop on Main - Book One

The Memory Box - Book Two

The Christmas Cottage - A Holiday Novella (Book 2.5)

The Letter - Book Three

The Christmas Scarf - A Holiday Novella (Book 3.5)

The Magnolia Cafe - Book Four

The Unexpected Wedding - Book Five

The Wedding in the Grove (crossover short story between series - Josephine and Paul from The Letter.)

LIGHTHOUSE POINT ~ THE SERIES

Wish Upon a Shell - Book One

Wedding on the Beach - Book Two

Love at the Lighthouse - Book Three

Cottage near the Point - Book Four

Return to the Island - Book Five

Bungalow by the Bay - Book Six

SWEET RIVER ~ THE SERIES

A Dream to Believe in - Book One

A Memory to Cherish - Book Two

A Song to Remember - Book Three

INDIGO BAY ~ a multi-author series of sweet romance

Sweet Sunrise - Book Three

Sweet Holiday Memories - A short holiday story

Sweet Starlight - Book Nine

ABOUT THE AUTHOR

Kay writes sweet, heartwarming stories that are a cross between women's fiction and contemporary romance. She is known for her charming small towns, quirky townsfolk, and enduring strong friendships between the women in her books.

Kay lives in the Midwest of the U.S. and can often be found out and about with her camera, taking a myriad of photographs which she likes to incorporate into her book covers. When not lost in her writing or photography, she can be found spending time with her ever-supportive husband, knitting, or playing with her puppies —two cavaliers and one naughty but adorable Australian shepherd. Kay and her husband also love to travel. When it comes to vacation time, she is torn between a nice trip to the beach or the mountains—but the mountains only get considered in the summer—she swears she's allergic to snow.

Learn more about Kay and her books at kaycorrell.com

While you're there, sign up for her newsletter to hear about new releases, sales, and giveaways.

WHERE TO FIND ME:
kaycorrell.com
authorcontact@kaycorrell.com

Join my Facebook Reader Group. We have lots of fun and you'll hear about sales and new releases first!
https://www.facebook.com/groups/KayCorrell/

facebook.com/KayCorrellAuthor

instagram.com/kay5

pinterest.com/kaycorrellauthor

amazon.com/author/kaycorrell

bookbub.com/authors/kay-correll